CYBER ARMAGEDDON

BOOK ONE: RISE OF THE LOCUSTS

MARK GOODWIN

Technical information in the book is included to convey realism. The author shall not have liability or responsibility to any person or entity with respect to any loss or damage caused, or allegedly caused, directly or indirectly by the information contained in this book.

All of the characters, places, and incidents are products of the author's imagination or are used fictitiously. Any resemblance to actual people, places, or events is entirely coincidental.

Copyright © 2018 Goodwin America Corp.

All rights reserved. No part of this publication may be reproduced, stored in a retrieval system, or transmitted in any form or by any means without the prior written permission of the author, except by a reviewer who may quote short passages in a review.

ISBN: 9781727896510

ACKNOWLEDGMENTS

I would like to thank my Editor in Chief Catherine Goodwin, as well as the rest of my fantastic editing team, Jeff Markland, Frank Shackleford, Stacey Glemboski, Sherrill Hesler, Paul Davison, Carole Pickard, and Claudine Allison.

PROLOGUE

The heads thereof judge for reward, and the priests thereof teach for hire, and the prophets thereof divine for money: yet will they lean upon the Lord, and say, Is not the Lord among us? none evil can come upon us.

Micah 3:11

In 2010 the NSA's Operation Olympic Games changed the face of cyberwarfare and cyberespionage forever. In coordination with the Israelis, The National Security Agency's program developed the most advanced and complex piece of malware code ever created. The weaponized code has come to be known as the Stuxnet virus. Stuxnet attacked Iran's nuclear-enrichment centrifuges and severely delayed the rogue nation's ability to produce a nuclear weapon. The Stuxnet virus not only disabled the centrifuges, but by attacking the SCADA systems which controlled the machinery, made them spin out of control causing physical damage to the hardware. The attack permanently disabled the equipment, to the point that the centrifuges were no longer usable.

This event was considered a major win for both the US and Israel. Just as Hiroshima and Nagasaki proved nuclear superiority for America, Stuxnet had established the US as the leader in cyberwarfare and cyberespionage. Yet, just as it didn't take long for other nations to develop the technology and enter the atomic arms race, mimicking the Stuxnet attack will take even less time.

Unlike the science required to develop a nuclear warhead, Stuxnet left behind the code used to initiate the attack, providing a blueprint for enemy nation states to reverse engineer the virus. By now, it is likely that all of America's adversaries possess malicious cyber programs similar in complexity to the Stuxnet exploit.

Few news items challenged the preeminence of the Stuxnet virus in the cyber world until 2017. In April of that year, a group known as the Shadow Brokers announced that they had obtained leaked hacking tools developed by the NSA and would be making them available to hackers worldwide. Two of the hijacked exploits were called EternalBlue and DoublePulsar. These two programs were used by hackers to develop the WannaCry ransomware attack, which targeted computers running Windows operating systems in May of 2017.

WannaCry infected some 200 thousand machines in 150 countries. The exploit wreaked havoc across the world, bringing down the National Health Services in England and Scotland. Nissan and Renault both had to cease manufacturing automobiles as a result of the attack. FedEx shipping was disrupted worldwide as was Spain's telecommunication capabilities and Germany's transportation system.

The virus disrupted the Russian postal service as well as several Russian banks, which helped to quell the rumors suggesting Russia's FSB had created the malicious code; but then again, what better way could a nation-state put on a guise of innocence? Such is the nature of cyber-attacks. A smoking gun rarely exists. At the end of the day, conjecture and finger-pointing make poor substitutes for hard evidence.

Before stepping down from her role as Homeland Security Secretary, Janet Napolitano warned that a cyber 9/11 was imminent. Former CIA Director James Woolsey has also been very vocal in issuing caveats about the likelihood of a massive cyber-attack; the likes of which could bring down critical infrastructure such as the electrical grid, communications, water systems, as well as major banking institutions. Additionally, former Director of National Intelligence James Clapper warned that America faces a coming Cyber Armageddon.

The story in this book is fiction, but the threat is

very real. Plan accordingly.

CHAPTER 1

The great day of the Lord is near, it is near, and hasteth greatly, even the voice of the day of the Lord: the mighty man shall cry there bitterly. That day is a day of wrath, a day of trouble and distress, a day of wasteness and desolation, a day of darkness and gloominess, a day of clouds and thick darkness, a day of the trumpet and alarm against the fenced cities, and against the high towers. And I will bring distress upon men, that they shall walk like blind men, because they have sinned against the Lord: and their blood shall be poured out as dust, and their flesh as the dung. Neither their silver nor their gold shall be able to deliver them in the day of the Lord's wrath; but the whole land shall be devoured by the fire of his jealousy: for he shall make even a speedy riddance of all them that dwell in the land.

Zephaniah 1:14-18

The smell of burning rubber filled the midnight air in the Atlanta suburb of Buckhead. The orange blaze of distant fires reflected from the clouds in the dark sky above the city. Sirens pierced through the crisp atmosphere. Their high-pitched screams seemed to roar out of nowhere then fade to near silence. But the silence never came. By the time the sound of one emergency vehicle had dwindled to a hush, another quickly took its place.

Standing next to her car, Kate McCarthy pulled a box of shotgun shells out of her pack. She put five shells in her left front pocket and placed the rest in the center console of her Mini Countryman. She pulled back her long blonde hair into a ponytail and fished it through the opening of her ball cap. She lowered the bill of the cap, then positioned the pump-action shotgun between the console and the passenger's seat.

Kate opened the trunk of her vehicle. "Vicky, you and your brother are riding with me. You can put your bags in here."

Fourteen-year-old Victoria looked stressed as she hoisted her belongings into the back of her Aunt Kate's car.

Sixteen-year-old Samuel dropped his pack next to his sister's suitcase. "What about mom? Is she coming?"

Sam's father, Terry, pressed his lips and closed the back of his Escalade. "I don't know, son. I begged her, but she'll have to make that decision for herself. Either way, you guys are coming with us."

"I don't want to leave mom here alone." Sam walked back into the house. "I'm going to talk to her."

Kate put her hand on her niece's shoulder. "Let's go ahead and get in the car."

Vicky watched her brother go back into the house but did as her aunt asked. "Yeah, okay."

Terry glanced at his watch then looked back up at his sister.

Kate smiled nervously, hating the situation and disliking the fact that her sister-in-law was putting Terry in such a terrible position.

Minutes later, Sam came out the front door. "Mom's coming! She's coming with us."

Terry gave a sigh of relief. "Good job, son."

"She just needs to pack a few things."

Terry shook his head. "No. We've gotta go now."

"Dad, she has to bring clothes. You have to give her some time."

"Five minutes. No more."

Vicky sunk low in the back seat of Kate's car. "I hate this. I don't care if we stay or go, but I just wish they could get along."

Kate powered on the walkie-talkies and carried one of the hand-held units up to her brother's

Escalade. "Push to talk. The channels are set. If you accidentally change it, go back to channel three."

"Got it." Terry pressed the talk button. "Check, check, check." His voice came through loud and clear on Kate's radio.

Five minutes passed yet there was no sign of Terry's wife, Penny.

"What's taking her so long?" Terry clenched his jaw.

"She's a woman. It takes us a little longer." Kate tried to ease the situation.

"I wish she'd thought of that when I asked her to pack a bag eight hours ago."

"But you're glad she decided to come." Kate rubbed Terry's shoulder.

He sighed. "I'm glad she decided to come."

Nearly twenty minutes had passed when Sam reemerged from the house with two of his mother's suitcases in tow. "She'll be right out."

Terry quickly assisted Sam with loading the bags into the Escalade.

"I really don't understand why we couldn't wait until morning. This is very absurd, running off in the cover of night." Penny lugged yet another large bag for Terry to load into the vehicle.

"Get in!" Terry shut the rear of the vehicle and rushed to the driver's seat.

Kate hurried to her car. She looked in the rearview at her niece and nephew. "Buckle up."

"Let me know when you're ready," Terry's voice came over the walkie-talkie.

"All set." Kate placed the radio next to the shotgun shells and put the car in drive.

Terry led the way, driving quickly. He called over the radio. "We'll take Lake Forest north. It runs parallel to US-19 but will have much less traffic. Once we pass I-285, we'll be through the worst of it and can get on 19."

Kate pressed the talk key. "Sounds good." With each passing block, she felt an increasing sense of relief. Every mile put her small caravan further and further from the chaos erupting in Atlanta. Kate watched the rearview and the ominous scarlet glimmers from the individual fires melt into a solitary halo of ruby over the metropolis.

Vicky leaned forward. "What was that old saying about the weather grandpa used to say? Something about red sky at night, sailors delight?"

Sam corrected her. "Yeah, but it's 1:30 AM. So, technically, it would be red sky in the morning, sailor take warning."

"Thanks for reminding me." Vicky slouched back in her seat.

Half an hour later, the convoy passed through Alpharetta and the landscape became more rural. Kate breathed easier. Few other motorists were on the road.

Sam commented, "Maybe the middle of the night is the best time to get out of Dodge after all."

Kate shook her head. "I'm not so sure about that. I think we've just been lucky."

"So far," Vicky added.

"True, but we are out of Atlanta. It should be smooth sailing from here on out." Kate let herself relax a little more. She followed the red lights of Terry's Escalade. She glanced at the side-view mirror to see a vehicle coming up from behind. Kate pressed the talk key on the radio. "I'm sure it's nothing, but this guy is coming up really fast from behind."

"I see him," Terry replied.

Kate watched as a heavy-duty Georgia Power work truck zoomed past her. The monster vehicle swerved in front of Terry causing him to veer off the side of the road. Kate slammed her brakes.

Time froze while she witnessed the careening Escalade leave the pavement in slow motion. She watched Terry's vehicle flip side over side twice. The SUV landed on its tires then rolled into the brush until it came to a complete stop, lodged between two trees.

Vicky shrieked with horror!

Sam yelled out at the top of his lungs. "Mom! Dad!"

Kate stopped on the shoulder of the road and rushed toward the SUV. She arrived at the crash site with her niece and nephew close behind. "Terry? Can you hear me?"

Her brother's face was bleeding, resting against the airbag. The driver's side door was wedged against the tree. She could not open it.

Terry looked up with a dazed expression.

"Take it easy, we'll get you out," declared Kate.

"They're coming back," Vicky screeched.

Terry seemed to come around to the danger at hand. He yelled through the window. "Get the kids and hide in the woods!"

"Maybe they're coming to help," suggested Sam.

"Go! Hide now!" Terry screamed through the

glass.

Unwillingly, Kate grabbed Vicky's hand. "Come on. Do as your father asked." She sprinted to her vehicle and grabbed the shotgun, then pushed her niece and nephew into the cover of the trees.

From the concealment of the woods, Kate watched the work truck come to a complete stop. It was a two-door bucket truck. Two armed men jumped out from each door. Two more had been riding on the back of the truck by the bucket boom. They also had weapons. None of them looked like Georgia Power employees. She figured they'd stolen the vehicle.

The man who came out of the driver's seat approached the Escalade. "Let's see what we've got."

One who had been riding in the rear examined Kate's Mini. "Looks like whoever was driving this one ran off. Think we should hunt them down?"

"If you want to tromp through the forest all night chasing someone in the dark, be my guest," replied the driver. "Besides, that's a girl's car. No self-respecting man would drive a thing like that. Probably the driver's daughter. She ain't gonna be no problem."

"Is he still alive?" asked another.

"Who knows. Go ahead and put a couple rounds through the windshield to be sure."

Kate's already-racing heart began to beat even faster. She knew she had one chance to save her brother. She motioned for the teen siblings to go farther into the forest. "This is about to get ugly. Get back and lie down," she whispered.

Reluctantly, they complied.

"The passenger doesn't look good neither. Go ahead and give her a couple rounds while you're at it," said the driver.

Kate raised the shotgun putting the front bead on the man who was about to kill Terry. Her hands shook with terror, her stomach constricted.

BOOOOM!

CHAPTER 2

What the chewing locust left, the swarming locust has eaten; what the swarming locust left, the crawling locust has eaten; and what the crawling locust left, the consuming locust has eaten. Awake, you drunkards, and weep; and wail, all you drinkers of wine, because of the new wine, for it has been cut off from your mouth.

For a nation has come up against My land, strong, and without number; his teeth are the teeth of a lion, and he has the fangs of a fierce lion. He has laid waste My vine, and ruined My fig tree; he has stripped it bare and thrown it away; its branches are made white. Lament like a virgin girded with sackcloth for the husband of her youth.

Joel 1:4-8

One week earlier.

Kate hustled across the busy downtown street. She wore a sharp, blue-with-white-pinstriped skirt suit, thick black-rimmed glasses, and her long blonde hair was pulled back into a no-nonsense ponytail. She put her purse on the Oak Wood Café patio table. "Sorry, I'm running late."

Her brother stood and embraced her. "No worries. I'm just glad you could make it."

Kate took her seat and Terry pushed her chair in. It was late September and the scorching Atlanta heat had finally subsided enough to eat lunch outside. The restaurant bustled with activity; hostesses, patrons, and servers zoomed by. Oak Wood was a favorite spot for the two siblings who both worked in the towering skyscraper across the street. At 870 feet, Sky National Plaza was the second tallest building in Atlanta.

"What are you going to have?" Terry looked over the menu.

Kate's eyes flicked up at the waiter who'd just arrived, pen in hand. "I suppose I'll have the sea bass. And a double espresso."

"I'll take the steelhead trout and a side of mac and cheese." Terry passed his menu to the server, turning his attention to Kate. "Up all night playing video games again?"

"Good guess, but not this time. I'm in

information security. Just because I work at a bank doesn't mean I get the privilege of working banker's hours."

Terry grinned. "I might be in financial services, but I'm pretty sure none of the departments at Sky National are required to work double shifts."

Kate felt tired and allowed herself to relax in the chair. "I picked up the graveyard shift for Marsha last night. Her grandmother is in the hospital. It might be the last chance she has to say goodbye."

"That was kind of you. Does her grandmother live around here?"

"No. She's down in Valdosta."

"Here's your espresso, Ma'am."

Kate took the small cup from the waiter. "Thanks. You can go ahead and bring me another one of these."

She took a sip of the thick black concoction. "How are Penny and the kids?"

Terry crossed his arms and looked up. "Penny is good. The kids keep her busy. Sam has his learner's permit. Vicky has some guy calling the house."

"No way!" Kate scowled. "She's too young!"

Terry raised his shoulders. "I know, but what am I going to do?"

"Shut it down, that's what."

"Then the guy becomes forbidden fruit. She'll like him that much more. I have to trust that we've brought her up right, that she'll make the right decisions."

Kate waved her hand. "Yeah, don't listen to me. I'm just jealous because I'm 34 and no guys are calling my house."

"I don't believe that. What about the guy in your department? Don't you play video games with him?"

"Albert? Nope! He's a good IS worker and a good teammate for Black Ops, but that's where my interest ceases."

"Black Ops?"

"Yeah, it's an online multiplayer video game. He plays at his house and I play at mine. I like it that way."

The server brought their food and they began eating.

"You're sure about Albert? I know you've had issues in the past where you let your social-anxiety thing get in the way of your happiness."

"No, I'm positive. I feel completely comfortable around Albert, which is good for a friend, but if I like a guy, I'm a wreck. He just doesn't do it for me."

Terry finished chewing. "Nobody on the scene does it for you? What about that guy you met at the hackers' conference in Vegas? What's the name of it?"

"The conference is called DefCon." She let her fork rest on her plate. "The guy's name is Gavin. He emailed me. We play Titanfall together and chat online, but we stick to talking about gaming."

"He never asked for your phone number?"

She frowned. "He did."

"And you said no."

"I did." She looked down at her plate.

"You have to be brave, Sis. I know it's risky, but you have to take a chance."

She shook her head. "Not with Gavin. He's not the type of guy who would be interested in me anyway."

"What are you talking about? He asked for your number."

"Yeah, but just to talk about gamer stuff."

"Come on, Sis. Guys don't ask for girls' telephone numbers just to talk about video games."

"You don't understand, I clam up, my heart races, I stutter and shake, my mouth goes dry, it's terrible. The alternative is that I say nothing, then guys think I'm rude or distracted."

"Are you still taking Jiu-Jitsu? You said you thought that might help build your confidence."

"I am and it is; at least in general. Knowing that you can choke someone out makes them less intimidating. But it doesn't work with cute guys and authority figures. Choking *them* out wouldn't usually help matters."

Terry smiled. "You're fitting in nicely at work."

"Probably because they all know I'm your sister."

"I have no clout in IS. My name means nothing there."

"It got me a job."

"No, it got you an interview. Your experience got you the job. Besides, that was just an HR thing."

"The director of IS asked about you when I got called into the office over that penetration testing exercise I initiated. I have a feeling I would have been in a lot more trouble if I hadn't been your little sister."

"They called me about that one. You scared

some people."

"They needed to be scared. IS is tasked with keeping the network secure, but there's only so much you can do if people aren't practicing safe online habits."

"Kate, you hacked the top systems administrator of Sky National Bank and somehow had the email password of the CFO."

"Private consulting firms would have charged fifty thousand dollars to a company like Sky National to perform that level of penetration testing. I did it for free and got reprimanded for it."

Terry nodded slightly. "But you embarrassed people. There's a way to handle things like that. Still, you're right. It's what you do and you're good at it. They should have realized that you were doing them a favor."

She finished her espresso and started on the second cup which the waiter had left on the table. "It's fine by me. I'll just do my job and spend the weekends hunting bugs."

"Does that pay well? I mean if you identify a vulnerability as a freelancer?"

"It depends on the company. Google, Facebook, and some of the big tech security firms shell out fairly large bounties if you find a bug. But every bug hunter out there is gunning for the big prizes. I usually pick the low-hanging fruit. The payoff is only a couple hundred bucks, but less competition."

"How do you find companies willing to pay for hacking them?"

"There's a website called bugcrowd.com. It lists who will pay out bounties."

"So, how did you hack Sky National?"

"Look around us." Kate turned from side to side. "Half the people in this restaurant work at Sky National Bank. I brought a backpack with a cell phone jammer and a device called a pineapple. The pineapple piggybacks off of Oak Wood Café's WiFi and acts as a hotspot. Once people can't use their cell carrier to check their email or social media, they have to use the café's WiFi. When they log on via my pineapple's hotspot, I can see everything they're doing; including passwords."

Terry's mouth hung open in disbelief. "It's that easy? How do you know they'll log on via your device? Why wouldn't they just use Oak Wood's regular WiFi?"

"Social engineering basically. Oak Wood's WiFi is named 'Oak Wood Guest.' I named the spoofed WiFi 'Oak Wood High Speed.' People think they're logging into the management's account or something, think they're getting one over on somebody. It makes them feel smart and technologically savvy."

Listening, Terry pressed his tongue in his cheek. "Unbelievable."

Kate's phone rang. "Hold on, I have to take this."

She held her phone to her ear. "Hey, Albert, what's up?"

"Everything is going crazy. Multiple accounts are being drained. I tried to issue a stop payment. I ordered the receiving banks to redeposit the funds, but the money is already gone."

Kate jumped up from her chair. "Take the system

down. Do it now!"

"But all of our customers will be locked out of their accounts," Albert protested.

"Their money will still be there when we go back online. Albert, we've been owned. Take us offline, right now!"

"Okay."

Kate listened to the sound of Albert's fingers clicking against the keyboard. She looked at her brother. "Sorry, I've gotta go. This isn't good."

"Do what you have to do. I've got the check."

"Thanks!" She grabbed her purse and sprinted across the street to the office tower.

CHAPTER 3

The field is wasted, the land mourneth; for the corn is wasted: the new wine is dried up, the oil languisheth. Be ye ashamed, O ye husbandmen; howl, O ye vinedressers, for the wheat and for the barley; because the harvest of the field is perished. The vine is dried up, and the fig tree languisheth; the pomegranate tree, the palm tree also, and the apple tree, even all the trees of the field, are withered: because joy is withered away from the sons of men. Gird yourselves, and lament, ye priests: howl, ye ministers of the altar: come, lie all night in sackcloth, ye ministers of my God: for the meat offering and the drink offering is withholden from the house of your God.

Joel 1:10-13

Kate held her ID badge over the sensor to unlock the door and rushed into the Information Security Control Center. The ambient light of the large monitors, which lined the walls overhead, provided most of the illumination in the room. In order to reduce glare on the screens, dim lights above aimed at the soft tiles on the ceiling, reflecting down in a gentle glow.

Albert and the other IS analysts stood motionless, staring at the screens. Kate needed no affirmation that the bank's system had been taken offline. The monitors above her head, which usually streamed with constant flows of data, displayed a static image. She'd never seen the large open room so still, nor heard it so quiet. Neither had she felt the sense of impending doom hanging like a dark cloud above the space in which she'd spent so much of her time over the past two years.

Albert turned to face her. He adjusted his glasses and frowned.

Kate pressed her lips together tightly. "Did you call Don?"

"He called here."

She rolled her eyes. "Great."

Albert scratched his head nervously. "He said for you to call him right away."

"Let's get this over with." Kate sighed and walked up the stairs to her glass-enclosed office; although, it wasn't exactly *her* office. The transparent elevated workspace, which looked over all the analysts on the floor, belonged to the IS shift supervisor. It was hers for now, but once she clocked out, the office which had been given the pejorative moniker, the *Crystal Palace*, by the security analysts, would belong to someone else. She realized what a nerdy name it was, but like herself, IS personnel were the type of people who liked writing code, studying algorithms, watching sci-fi, and reading epic fantasy novels. Their peculiar culture lent itself to such nicknames.

Kate hated the room. She'd looked upon her predecessors as smug authoritarians and was sure her co-workers saw her the same way. But, the salary was nearly double what she was paid as an analyst. She wondered if it was worth it. Kate picked up the receiver to call the Sky National Chief Information Security Officer Don Lombardo.

She'd known the CISO for over a year but still felt nervous when speaking with him. "Mr. Lombardo, hi, it's Kate."

"Where were you?"

"I went to lunch. I came back right away, sir."

"You're the person in charge of securing $210 billion in assets. You can't leave when you're the shift supervisor."

"It's never been a problem before, sir. Albert watches the floor while I go to lunch and take breaks. He has the same level of security clearance as me. He's even been shift supervisor before."

"Well, we've never had a breach like we had today, so that all changes, effective immediately!"

"Yes, sir."

"We lost over $3 million in a matter of seconds. And every minute we stay offline, the bigger this problem is getting. We're bleeding customer confidence, which is the very life force of a bank. Find the breach, patch it, and get us back up and running as soon as humanly possible."

"Yes, sir." Kate heard Lombardo hang up abruptly. She wasn't offended by his rudeness, rather she was happy the conversation had been terminated so readily. It gave her a moment to focus. She stared out at the frozen monitors encrusting the wall before her, like glowing scales on a great dragon. Her mind raced to develop a game plan. She considered the talents of the individual analysts on the floor and parsed out the unique tasks required to get the system secured and back online. Kate allowed herself a full minute to review her strategy before emerging from the Crystal Palace. She pushed the door open and stood on the catwalk above the analysts. "Albert, put a trace on the money that was taken out of the accounts. Find out where the money went. If it was used to purchase goods or services, initiate stop payments. If it was used to purchase cryptocurrencies, get the information of the purchaser, especially if it was in a country that has Know-Your-Customer laws. If so, report it to the appropriate authorities. We'll never get it all back, but if we can claw back a reasonable amount, even 25 percent, it will make us all look a lot better.

"Linda, run an analysis on the nature of the hacks. Find any similarities that you can. Look for commonalities in the people whose accounts were hacked as well as any correlation between the IP addresses of the hackers.

"Quinton, work with Linda and look over the data that she pulls. Figure out if this is an internal or an external breach.

"Rodney, begin a level-three security reset protocol. Put us back online and require a password change for all online banking customers, complete with a one-time email or text authentication code.

Albert looked up at her and shook his head. "Don isn't going to like that."

Kate made her way toward the stairs to join her team in the recovery effort. "We don't have any other options. It's the only way we can go back online without risking more money being stolen."

Half an hour later, Kate got a text.

Albert looked over her shoulder. "Zachery Mendoza. If I was going to get balled out, I'd rather hear it from Zach than Don."

She twisted her mouth to one side. "He wants me to call him."

"At least we're back up and running. You'll have some good news to give him."

She looked up from her phone at Albert. "Keep working on the recovery efforts. Text me if you get any more money back. Even though this wasn't our fault, our department is the one that is going to take the heat."

"Sure thing, boss." He smirked.

"And don't call me *boss*." She stomped off to the stairs.

"Whatever you say, boss."

She grunted her displeasure and continued up to her office.

Kate dialed the number for Sky National Chief Data Officer Zachery Mendoza.

"Hello?"

She felt anxious speaking to anyone she didn't know well, especially an authority figure. "Mr. Mendoza, hi, it's Kate McCarthy from IS."

"Hey, Kate. Thanks for calling. We're putting together a briefing for the board tomorrow morning and I need you to come by my office and give me a first-hand account of what happened today."

Speaking to the man on the phone was bad enough, but a face-to-face meeting would push her to a borderline panic attack. "Can I explain it over the phone? We're still sort of mopping up the mess around here. Although, we do have the network back online. Customers have full access to all of Sky National Bank's services; that includes banking and investment accounts. We've also recovered about $200 thousand of the stolen funds."

"Good work, Kate. I don't want to pull you away from your responsibilities. Finish your shift, then come by."

"It could be late when I get out. I'll have to debrief the incoming shift supervisor."

"It's going to be a late one for all of us. I'll see you when you get here."

"Sure. I'll see you then, Mr. Mendoza." She grimaced and hung up the phone.

It was after 7:00 PM when Kate finally finished for the evening. She spent a few minutes rehearsing what she'd say to the CDO when she arrived in his office. Being prepared before a meeting was one of her limited techniques for controlling her jitters. She took the elevator to the 58th floor where Mendoza's office was located. On the ride up, Kate practiced her breathing exercises to calm her nerves. She counted to four slowly, inhaled through her nose, held the breath for four counts. Kate then steadily released the breath, counting to four once again.

The elevator doors opened and Kate stepped out. She approached the secretary's desk. "Hi, I'm here to see Mr. Mendoza."

"You're Kate from IS?"

"Yes."

"Go right in."

Kate smiled at the secretary, then opened the door. Inside was no less than five C-level administrators. She felt her anxiety threatening to make her freeze in her tracks. Her first instinct was to turn around and run. She could email a resignation letter in the morning and return to hunting for bug bounties in the comfort of her own apartment. But she couldn't do that to Terry who'd gone out on a limb to get her the job. She had to be strong for him, and she had to be strong for herself.

Kate walked into the room. Don Lombardo glowered at her. His voice seemed to blame her while he introduced her to the others sitting around Mendoza's office. "Gentlemen, this is Kate McCarthy, she was the supervisor who was *supposed* to be on the floor when we were breached this afternoon."

"Supposed to be?" Sky National Bank CEO

Xavier Altoviti looked at Kate for clarification.

She glanced at her feet to avoid Lombardo's accusatory glare. She pulled her arms over her chest as if to protect herself from the steely daggers she felt would surely come next. Kate forced herself to look the CEO in the eyes. "Yes, sir. I'd stepped out to have lunch with my brother. I left Albert Rodgers in charge while I was away. He called me immediately when the breach occurred. I ordered him to shut down the network so we could stem the bleeding. He complied. I'm not sure what else I could have done even if I'd been present, sir."

Altoviti said, "McCarthy. Is your brother Terry McCarthy?"

"Yes, sir."

"I love that guy. Kate, please sit down. And don't be nervous. We're not here to assign blame. We just need to find out what happened so we can address the board in the morning."

"Thank you." Altoviti's voice put her somewhat at ease. She took a seat as far away from Lombardo as possible.

Mendoza was the next to speak. "Kate, I know you've had a long day and must be tired. Why don't you walk us through what happened today, then you can go home and get some rest."

"Yes, sir." Kate proceeded to give a minute-by-minute accounting of all the events that had transpired since she received Albert's call during lunch. She explained all the data analysis her team had performed since the hack and her reasoning for initiating the level-three security reset protocol which had inconvenienced so many customers by making them change their passwords. She told how the team's initial findings indicated that the breach had likely been external but that multiple attacks had been carried out all at the same time to maximize the confusion element in the information security control center.

Mendoza rubbed his chin. "You said the breach was most likely external. So you think multiple customers were compromised individually to steal their login credentials, then the hackers hit all their accounts at once?"

"Yes, sir. It was likely rootkits installed on the customers' PCs through phishing emails. However, it's not clear how the perpetrators obtained the customer email list in the first place. Since we don't share customers' information with third parties that could have been the result of an internal breach."

Lombardo interjected. "Phishing scams are used to directly get passwords, not install rootkits."

Kate blinked toward Lombardo, then back to the CEO. "It's increasingly popular to use phishing type emails that mimic correspondence from banking institutions like Sky National which have clickable links in the body of the message. Once the customer clicks the link, the rootkit installs and gives the hacker access to the infected device. That's why our system didn't detect that the accounts were being accessed by new devices. All of the fraudulent transactions were made by the victims' home computers."

"Doesn't anti-virus software protect against that kind of stuff?" CFO Nick Hampton asked.

"Not if it's a zero-day, sir," Kate answered.

"What's a zero-day?" Hampton inquired.

"It's a threat which hasn't been identified by any cyber security firm yet. It has been protected against by anti-virus software for zero-days," she said.

"So have we found the bug? Can we keep this from happening again?" Mendoza asked.

"Not yet. I've spoken to several of the victims over the phone and many of them have granted me remote access to their computers. I have friends in the cyber-security industry who are willing to help me find the malicious code." Kate crossed her hands.

Lombardo stood up. "Oh, no. You're not bringing in outside contractors. We have to keep a tight lid on this thing. If word gets out that we had a breach this big, people will start pulling out of Sky National immediately. Then the stock price will get hit and the dominoes will just keep falling."

"Wait a minute, Don." Xavier Altoviti held up his hand and signaled for Lombardo to take his seat. "I want to hear what Ms. McCarthy has to say."

Lombardo sat down but continued to protest. "Mr. Altoviti, I can assure you this is a project that my department is more than capable of handling on our own. We don't need any help from outside firms."

The CEO tightened his jaw. "Don, I brought you on to this position because you had a very solid background in administration, even though you didn't really possess the technical knowledge that a CISO would typically bring to the table. I had expected that you'd study up and get proficient with information security, but I'm beginning to realize that it takes a certain personality type who understands the nature of the risks inherent to the modern age of total connectivity. I may have asked too much of you. I want to take ownership of that mistake."

"Not at all, sir." Lombardo piped down and shut his mouth.

Kate understood what Altoviti had said to Lombardo to be boardroom speak for *start getting your resume together*. She tried not to let her amusement show over Lombardo's dressing-down. Instead, she humbly said, "It wouldn't be outside contractors, sir. These are personal acquaintances of mine who would respect our need for confidentiality."

The CEO said, "Okay, I'll green-light that operation. But please, make sure everyone in your department understands that we have to keep this close to our chest. We haven't figured out how we're going to handle this just yet. If we take it to the FDIC, the breach immediately goes public. Just what we'd lose in the stock price could easily eclipse what was stolen, not to mention lost revenue from a severe cut in our customer base. Heck, we'd probably shell out more in damage control than what was siphoned off in today's attack. Our in-house PR department couldn't contain a mess this big."

CFO Nick Hampton added, "We've got a rainy-day fund that could cover most of today's losses."

Kate hesitated but finally said, "It's not much, but I'm confident we'll be able to recover at least another $100 thousand."

Chief Data Officer Zachery Mendoza turned to Kate. "We appreciate your offer to have your friends look into the malicious code, but what's in it for them?"

She blushed. "They . . . well, we, I should say, are a bunch of computer nerds who are into that kind of thing. It's sort of a game to us. One gets a certain level of street cred in our community for being the first to identify a virus like this."

Mendoza grinned. "We're fortunate to have you at Sky National Bank."

Xavier Altoviti snapped his fingers. "Wait a minute, aren't you the girl who hacked Nick's email earlier this year?"

Kate's heart stopped and her mouth went dry. She looked down at her fingers which were nervously interlaced. "Yes, sir."

Altoviti began laughing. "I thought so." He turned to Nick Hampton. "Nick was all shaken up over that little prank, but I'll admit, I got a kick out of it."

"I assure you, sir. It was not intended as a prank." Her voice cracked.

The CEO stood up and walked over to her. He sat next to her and put his hand on her back. "Relax, Kate. We weren't expecting it, that's all. But you were right. You mentioned that the customer email list could have been obtained via an internal breach." Altoviti looked around the room. "Maybe if we'd paid attention to you back then, today's debacle could have been avoided altogether."

She looked up at Xavier Altoviti.

His eyes met hers. "Once the smoke clears from

this train wreck, I'd like you to put together a corporate memo on habits we can form that will keep the bank safer in the future. Will you do that for me? I'll make sure you're well compensated for your efforts."

"Of course, I will, Mr. Altoviti." She'd just gone from thinking she was about to be fired to getting what amounted to an unofficial promotion. Her emotions were raw; and between the double shift and the extra hours, she'd just worked nineteen hours straight. She welcomed the adjournment of the meeting and looked forward to her soft, comfortable bed.

CHAPTER 4

Alas for the day! for the day of the Lord is at hand, and as a destruction from the Almighty shall it come.

Joel 1:15

Wednesday morning, Kate shut off her alarm clock and forced herself to get up. She was still exhausted from the previous day. Once out of bed, she checked the Wire app on her phone. Sure enough, she had a message from Gavin. Her heart sparked and she suppressed a grin. Connecting with him on the encrypted messaging service was a big leap for her.

I heard your bank had some technical difficulties yesterday. Wondering if we're still on to play Titanfall tonight.

Rise of the Locusts

She twisted her mouth to one side and messaged him back. *We're still on. Might have to work late so it could be after eight by the time I get online. Just a glitch at work. No big deal.*

Kate put her phone on the counter and turned on the television. She turned on the coffee maker and made herself a bagel with cream cheese for breakfast. She poured a glass of orange juice, paying little attention to the news until she noticed the Sky National Bank logo on the screen. She quickly grabbed her juice and bagel, making her way to the couch.

She put her breakfast on the glass-top coffee table and turned up the volume.

"Two million Sky National Bank customers were frozen out of their accounts yesterday afternoon in what a company spokesperson is calling a temporary service outage. Once customers were able to access the bank's website nearly an hour later, they were forced to reset their passwords and authenticate their identity via text or email. Some have speculated that the mega-bank may have experienced some type of security breach, but no concrete evidence has been provided to confirm the rumors."

Kate's phone buzzed. It was a message from Gavin. *Turn on CNN.*
She messaged back. *Already watching.*
Glitch?
She messaged back with a mouthless emoji.
Gavin responded. *We need to talk. Can I call*

you?

She froze up. Unable to respond. Kate practiced her breathing exercises for a few minutes.

You still there?

She braced herself and forced a reply. *Okay. When?*

Now?

Kate immediately wished she hadn't said okay. Certainly not now. She needed time. She had to prepare, to think about what she'd say, how she'd act. Talking to Gavin wasn't something she could just do on the spur of the moment. But what if she waited? The anxiety would build and it would hang like a cloud over her head all day, on a day that she needed to be more focused than ever. She messaged him back.

I've got to get ready for work. Can you give me twenty minutes? I can try to talk on the way to the office. This would give her an out if she got too frazzled. She'd blame it on heavy traffic which was a daily truth in downtown Atlanta.

What's your number?

She froze again. Why couldn't he just call her via the Wire app? If she gave him her number that was tantamount to saying that she liked him. She could never admit a thing like that, not to someone like Gavin. But even more frightening was the thought of seeming weird if she didn't give him her number. She typed it in and hoped he wouldn't call.

Kate rushed to get ready so she could be out the door and in her car before Gavin called; *if* he called.

Fifteen minutes later, she was in her blue Mini Countryman and on her way to the bank. The

Countryman offered all-wheel drive and slightly more room than the typical Mini Cooper. Kate purchased it for the rare Atlanta snowstorm and her annual pilgrimage to the Waynesville, North Carolina cabin on four acres, which her father had left to her and her two brothers. Terry always took his family to the cabin for Christmas. Kate joined them each December. Her younger brother, Boyd, typically did not.

Her phone rang and she braced herself for the uncomfortable ordeal of talking directly to a guy that she really liked. She pressed the speaker so she could talk and drive. "Hello?"

"Kate, I can't believe I'm actually talking to you on the phone."

"What's the big deal? You talked to me at DefCon. And we talk to each other in Titanfall."

"Yeah, but this is different. When you shot me down at DefCon I didn't think I'd ever get your number."

"I didn't shoot you down."

"You wouldn't give me your number. But that's cool. I understand, you probably have a boyfriend or whatever. Anyway, I just wanted to know if you could tell me anything about what happened at work. Since I work in information security at Bank of America, I was wondering if there's anything I should be looking out for. I mean let's be honest, I know it wasn't just a glitch."

She was quiet for a moment.

"Hello? Are you still there?"

"I don't have a boyfriend." Immediately, she regretted her awkward reply.

Now Gavin's end of the phone was silent.

She attempted to redirect the conversation which was quickly coming off the rails. "I mean, that's not why I wouldn't give you my number. It's just that I barely knew you."

"Yeah, sure. Whatever." Now Gavin sounded nervous. "I totally understand."

Kate composed herself. "I guess it would be prudent to have all your customers reset their passwords."

"Okay, so it wasn't a glitch."

"I thought you already knew that."

"Not for sure, but I do now."

She blew out a deep breath. "I can't say much else about it."

"I totally get that."

"Unless."

"Unless what?"

"We haven't identified the malicious code. I have permission to share access to the infected computers with trusted people who have the skills to find the banking Trojan and block it."

"What do you mean you haven't identified the code? Are you talking about a zero-day?"

"Yeah."

"No kidding! I'd love to get a chance to help find the virus. So, are you saying I'm trusted people?"

"I don't know. Are you?"

"I run the night shift for IS at Bank of America's corporate office here in Charlotte. I guess they think I am."

She'd loosened up considerably during the short conversation. "Yeah, but they'll hire anybody."

Rise of the Locusts

"Give me a break! So, am I in?"

"I'll have to think about it." She enjoyed teasing him, once her collywobbles died down. "Do you have Signal on your desktop? If we're going to talk, it has to be secure."

"I have Signal at work. I can install it on my machine at home. What time?"

"Is 6:00 good?"

"Yeah. I have to leave for work at 10:30 tonight, so I'll have a few hours."

"Okay, I'll talk to you then." She ended the call and felt a rush of exhilaration over the evening's coming online encounter.

Kate arrived at work a few minutes later. When she walked into the control center, she was met by Zachery Mendoza. "Mr. Mendoza, it's a pleasure to see you again."

"Thanks, Kate. You're still in charge today, but we've brought in a few extra people from IT who will assist your team with anything they might need. Until we can identify the malware, we can't be sure that we won't have subsequent breaches."

"You're correct, and we can certainly use the extra eyeballs watching for unusual activity." She looked at him. "Pardon me for asking, but wouldn't Mr. Lombardo typically be running oversight for information security?"

Mendoza cracked a grin and signaled for Kate to lead the way up the stairs to the Crystal Palace. "He would, but Don is taking a couple days off."

"At a time like this?" She glanced back before ascending the stairs.

"I'm not sure it was his decision."

"Oh." Kate knew better than to ask for more details.

Once they arrived in the upstairs office, Mendoza asked, "If Albert ran the floor today, would you be able to get a jump on going through those infected computers?"

"Sure."

"You mentioned yesterday that you might know some other people who could help us out. I looked over your resume. You listed that you'd done some freelance work, hunting for vulnerabilities; bug bounty hunting, I think it's called. Would that also be an accurate description of the people you were speaking of?"

Kate replied, "Yes, sir, but some of them would do it for the thrill."

"That's quite kind, but we'd like to add an incentive. If you can find the Trojan horse and block it, we'll pay you a $10,000 bonus. Plus, we'll pay $5,000 to each of the people who help you, up to twenty people."

"You're very generous, sir. But I doubt I know that many white-hat hackers. More like three or four."

"Very well. Is this office a good workstation?"

"Not really. I need a Linux machine, and I need a fast one."

"I'd be happy to get one for you."

"Getting it set up would take the better part of a day. I have a really good system at my apartment. It's configured for scanning code remotely. Would you have any objection to me working from home?"

"Not at all. What about your team? Will they

work from your place?"

She laughed, "No, they'll work remotely. Vijay, he's in Boston. He works for MIT. Then there's Shu, she's in San Francisco, and Willow is in Denver."

"So it will just be the four of you?"

Thinking about Gavin, she felt nervous. "I might have another guy on the project as well. He works for B of A, corporate HQ."

"In Charlotte?"

"Yes, sir."

"Okay. I trust your judgment. Do what you need to do, and I'll hold down the fort."

"Thank you, Mr. Mendoza." Kate left the office and made her way down to the floor.

Albert met her at the bottom of the stairs. "What's going on? We're tripping over these IT guys. They don't understand information security."

She rolled her eyes. "They understand it a little better than people from accounting would."

"Barely," he said snidely.

"Well, they're here to help, and you're in charge, so find them something to do."

Albert pushed his glasses up on his nose. "I'm in charge? Where are you going?"

"To look for the bug that caused this mess."

On her way home, Kate began calling all of her white-hat hacker friends. She called Vijay first, he would be the most excited about the opportunity. Being tenured in academia meant that Vijay could set aside his classes for a few days to pursue a pet project without being hassled.

Shu was next on Kate's list, knowing that she'd have to carve out some time from her tech-startup security consulting business.

And finally, there was Willow, an extremely smart trust-fund kid who did what she wanted, when she wanted, if she wanted.

Kate was home when she'd finished her three recruiting spiels. She had but one more call to make.

Once inside her apartment, she dialed Gavin's number.

"Hello." His voice sounded groggy.

"Hey, it's Kate. I'm sorry, did I wake you?"

"Yeah, I'm trying to find a zero-day exploit buried in who knows how many lines of code tonight, then I have to work the graveyard shift at the bank. I thought I might take a short nap. Tell me I didn't make a mistake by giving you my number. You're not an obsessive stalker, are you?"

Her face went hot, then cold, stunned at the accusation. "What? I gave you *my* number. I'm sorry I woke you, but don't flatter yourself, I'm not stalking you."

"Relax. I'm joking."

"Oh, right. Sure." She felt even more embarrassed at being so quick to defend herself.

He yawned. "Anyway, I couldn't get that lucky."

"Lucky how? To get a nap?"

"No, to get stalked by someone like you."

She recognized a quirky computer-geek compliment when she heard one, but figured he was probably still kidding around. "I just wanted to let you know that my boss let me leave early to start hunting the bug from home. I've talked to the rest of my team, and we're going to go ahead and get started."

"Who's the rest of your team?"

"Willow and Shu. They were the two girls with me at DefCon last month."

"Yeah, I remember them."

"And Vijay. He was at DefCon the year before but didn't make it this year."

"In that case, I better fire up my machine. I don't want this Vijay guy cutting in on my action."

Kate replied, "You don't have to worry about that. Regardless of who finds the bug we'll all share credit."

"That's not what I was talking about."

"I don't get it," she said.

"I don't want him putting the moves on you while I'm asleep."

"Ha, ha. Such a kidder." She desperately wanted him to clarify that he wasn't joking this time.

Gavin said, "I've got a case of Red Bull in the fridge for just such an emergency. Give me ten minutes, and I'll be online."

CHAPTER 5

Draw your water for the siege! Fortify your strongholds! Go into the clay and tread the mortar! Make strong the brick kiln! There the fire will devour you, the sword will cut you off; it will eat you up like a locust. Make yourself many—like the locust! Make yourself many—like the swarming locusts! You have multiplied your merchants more than the stars of heaven. The locust plunders and flies away.

Nahum 3:14-16 NKJV

Three hours had passed when the first Signal group video call came over Kate's computer. It was

Vijay.

"Hey, Vijay. Did you find something?" Kate asked.

He spoke with a thick Indian accent. "Maybe, but I would like to wait until everyone has joined the call."

Kate looked at the screen. "Looks like we're still waiting on Shu."

Willow said, "She sent me a text. She had to run out for a while. Something about one of her clients having security issues."

"Okay, in that case, I will begin," said Vijay.

"I wonder if Shu's thing is related to this." Gavin could be seen in one of the tiles on Kate's computer taking a long swig of his Red Bull. "New York's 911 emergency call system is out. We might be looking at something a little more large-scale than a simple bank heist."

"That is curious," said Kate. "Vijay, go ahead and tell us what you've got."

Vijay's video feed switched over to his screen flow. "Check out this huge chunk of code right here. It looks like a Windows update, but clearly it's not."

"Windows, huh?" Willow lowered her brow. "That takes some serious skills or an insider at Microsoft to pull that off."

"Maybe and maybe not," Gavin added.

"What do you mean?" Kate inquired.

He continued, "The NSA's DoublePulsar was designed to open up a backdoor into any Windows machine. Once a hacker has that kind of access, they can insert any kind of code they want. They can make it look like an update, a video file, or even part of the firmware antivirus system itself."

Willow said, "DoublePulsar was patched by Microsoft."

Gavin looked at the screen as if the statement was very naive. "And you think that's the only backdoor tool ever developed by the NSA?"

"Probably not," Willow admitted. "But it's the only one that was stolen."

"Correction," added Vijay. "It's the only one that we know about that was stolen. Even when the NSA knew their compromised toolkit was out there, they provided no guidance to security firms nor Microsoft themselves about what threats to protect against. The NSA has never been big on transparency."

"If something like that was out there, I'd think we would have heard about it," Willow said.

Kate considered the probability. "Not necessarily. DoublePulsar and EternalBlue were possibly just samples. The Shadow Brokers specifically said they had more NSA malware available for sale on the Darknet. I would imagine a state actor like China or Russia could cough up some pretty serious scratch for tools like that."

"Heck," Gavin added. "Kim Jong, Iran, or even Isis could afford some of those goodies."

Willow spoke again. "I've been looking through the Windows updates on the machine I was assigned to, and I've found a similar code." Her video feed switched to her screen flow. "Look at this line at the top. It's very similar to what Vijay found, but it's unique. If they're both viruses, technically they'd each be zero-days. Any anti-virus that would patch the vulnerability from what Vijay found would still let this piece of code through."

Kate shook her head in unbelief. "That's impossible. Can you imagine the time put into coding each one of these bugs? Who would waste two separate zero-days on the same attack?"

"Make that three." Gavin's video switched to his video feed. "Look what I found."

Kate read through lines of code. "Once again, completely unique."

Vijay spoke next. "The Trojans are incredibly simplistic in their design. I've never seen anything quite like it. They are very succinct, no filler except for what I would consider camouflage. This code must have been written by a genius."

"Or another computer," Willow commented.

"AI? I don't think so," said Gavin.

Willow continued, "Two guys who presented at DefCon 25 wrote a machine-learning program for hacking. Point number one, that was years ago. I'm sure even they have progressed in their research. Point number two, you guys don't think the NSA has developed AI for writing malware?"

Kate examined the codes and thought about Willow's premise. "Even if they had such a program, it would take a tremendous amount of computing power."

"Which they have," said Willow. "The NSA Data Center in Utah could easily accomplish such a task."

"Yeah, but the NSA wouldn't be running a program to steal a couple million dollars from a bank." Kate shook her head. "If such a program exists and has fallen into the wrong hands, it would take a state actor like China or Russia to operate it."

"Perhaps, not," Vijay said. "It might take time, but many more advanced colleges have the computing power to run an AI program of that magnitude."

Gavin spoke up. "You know who has command of lots of computing power, cryptocurrency engineers. They have people all over the world running programs which are supposedly solving problems to mine coins. What if rather than figuring out arbitrary math problems, all of these computers were actually running an AI program which was churning out all these bugs?"

"I don't think so," said Vijay. "I've seen the problems Bitcoin miners are solving. It's very complex stuff."

"Maybe not Bitcoin," Gavin replied, "but what about the hundreds of other cryptocurrencies?"

"I suppose it would be a possibility," Vijay yielded.

"I found the virus in the computer I'm inspecting." Kate toggled her feed so the others could see the code she was looking at. "Same thing. Very similar but it's a totally different bug. It's like a swarm of viruses; like a plague of locusts or something." She picked up her phone. "Guys, I'm going to sign off. I have to call this into the office. Thank you all so much for your help. Please message me if anyone gets an idea of how we can patch this."

Gavin snorted. "I've got an idea for a patch."

"What's that?" Kate listened intently.

"Pull all of your money out of the bank, cancel your credit cards, throw away your computer, and never go online again."

"I mean serious patches." She sighed.

"I am serious. This isn't good. We can't write a patch for every piece of computer hardware in the country. And if every machine has a unique bug, that's the only fix." Gavin's voice sounded grave.

Willow added, "And I hate to be the bearer of more bad news, but I just got an alert on my phone. Washington DC's subway system is offline. Sounds like the locusts are eating their way into every network in the country."

Kate started thinking about how far things could deteriorate. "Be safe guys. I'll speak with you all later."

"Okay, take care. I'm going to the grocery to stock up on some supplies." Gavin signed off.

Kate closed the Signal program on her desktop and grabbed her keys. She called Mr. Mendoza on the way out the door.

"Kate, hi. Did you find anything?"

"Yes, sir. But it's not good. I'm on my way to the office so I can discuss it with you. Also, I need to look around under the hood in our servers."

"Why? Do you think our network could be infected?"

"Whatever is going on is widespread. New York's emergency dispatch system is out, DC's trains aren't running, and my friend in San Francisco got called away for a cybersecurity emergency. I'm not sure what the nature of that threat is, but it's likely that all of this is connected to our breach." She opened the door of her Mini and got inside.

"I'll see you when you get here."

Kate raced across town to the office. She called Gavin on the way.

He answered, "I knew you were a stalker."

"Stop saying that!" she protested.

"I'm just dreaming. What's up?"

"Are you serious about buying extra groceries or were you just trying to freak everybody out?"

"They were all looking at the same code I saw. If that doesn't freak them out, nothing I say is going to do it. But yeah, I'm on the way to Harris Teeter right after I go to the bank."

"Why are you going to the bank? Are you going to talk to your boss about what's happening?"

"No. I'm going to take all of my money out. Or at least as much as they can give me on short notice."

"Gavin, you're overreacting."

"Okay."

"Okay?"

"Maybe you're right. If so, I'll put my money back in the bank when the smoke clears."

"But you can't take back a bunch of groceries." Kate tried to reason with him.

"No, but I gotta eat anyway. Worst case scenario, I have an extra hour in my schedule on grocery day for the next few months. I'm sure I'll figure out something to do with the spare time. I've always wanted to learn how to play cricket."

"It's a lot like baseball."

"Oh, then never mind. I hate baseball. Well, gotta go. I'm pulling into the bank parking lot right now. Can I call you from work tonight?"

"Yeah, sure."

"Great. I'll talk to you then."

She clicked off the phone. Kate hated the circumstances, but she was glad she'd found a way to connect with Gavin.

Suddenly, Kate slammed the brakes! Her car stopped inches away from the bumper of the car in front of her. The man in the vehicle ahead opened his door and yelled profanities at the car in front of him.

Kate looked up at the traffic light. It was green. She could see from beneath the louvers on the traffic signal for the cross traffic that it was also green. Six cars had collided in the intersection. "Great. I bet they've hacked the traffic signals." Kate looked around for a place to park. She was only about a mile from Sky National Bank Plaza and could walk there quicker if the traffic lights were going to be an on-going problem. She backed up to the last side street and cut over to Peachtree. "There's the Georgian. I can park at the hotel. It'll cost me, but at least my car will be safe."

She opted to pay extra for valet parking so she wouldn't have to waste even more time spiraling up and up to find an open space. Kate looked at her impractical shoes and growled. "I should keep sneakers in the car. I'm sure I will from now on." She began her long trek to the office.

On her way, she called her brother.

His receptionist picked up. "Hi, Kate. I'll put

you right through."

"Sis, hey. Did you get that thing worked out? I heard we had to go offline for a while yesterday and the big wigs called you in for your expert opinion."

"Yeah, I'm still working on it. That's what I wanted to talk to you about. Can you come by my place on your way home tonight?"

"Can't do it tonight. Penny has book club and Sam is going to the movies with his friends. I have to be home with Victoria."

"She's fourteen. I used to babysit when I was fourteen."

"It's a different world these days. I can't leave her at home alone. Why don't you drive out to the house?"

"Out to Buckhead?"

"It's nine miles."

She sighed. "Nine miles of chaos. You should see it out here. I had to leave my car at the Georgian. I'm walking the rest of the way to the office."

"Why? What happened?"

"The traffic lights are all messed up. I think it might be related to yesterday's hack. Did you hear about what's going on around the country?"

"I heard about the trains in DC and the 911 system in New York. You think they were hacked?"

"If not, it's an awfully big coincidence. You should ask Penny and Sam to stay home tonight."

"Yeah, right." Terry laughed. "That's not going to happen. So, are you coming by?"

"It might take me a while to get there, but I'll come. I gotta go. I'll see you tonight." She hung up the phone so she could pick up the pace to the office. She walked briskly past intersection after intersection of fender benders and enraged motorists, each blaming the others for the accidents.

CHAPTER 6

Blow ye the trumpet in Zion, and sound an alarm in my holy mountain: let all the inhabitants of the land tremble: for the day of the Lord cometh, for it is nigh at hand; A day of darkness and of gloominess, a day of clouds and of thick darkness, as the morning spread upon the mountains: a great people and a strong; there hath not been ever the like, neither shall be any more after it, even to the years of many generations.

Joel 2:1-2

    Kate sat scanning a computer screen at a desk in Zachery Mendoza's office on the 58th floor.

Mendoza watched over her shoulder. "Believe it or not, my Master's Degree is in Computer Science. I'd be glad to help if I knew what I was looking for."

"Our Microsoft SQL server is different from the infected personal PCs we went through earlier today, but I would expect to see some similarities if the bank's network is infected. However, I would not expect it to look like any type of an update."

"What if I brought in some more people to help? Would that speed things up?"

Kate looked up momentarily from her screen. "Albert is probably the only person on shift who is capable of processing enough information to be effective."

"Okay. I'll get him a workstation set up right over by the window. The three of us can scan code all night if we have to."

Kate looked up. "I have to go by my brother's tonight. It's super important. I can work until eight or so, but I've been staring at screens all day. I won't be very productive after that anyway. I can be back at 6:00 AM."

"That's fine. You're right. We have to get some rest. If we burn out, none of us will make any progress." Mendoza walked out of the office to speak to his secretary.

Kate, Albert, and Mendoza spent the next several hours examining line after line of code from the bank's mainframes, but to no avail.

At 8:00, Kate took off her glasses and rubbed her eyes. "Mr. Mendoza, we may be looking at code for the next two weeks. We may or may not find anything. I'm going to call it a night if you don't mind."

Mendoza looked up from his screen. "I'll let Janet know that you'll be using my office tomorrow. I'm going to keep looking for another couple of hours. I may be in late tomorrow."

"Okay. I'll be in early. Give me a call if you think you've found anything. Or better yet, take a picture of the screen and text it to me. I'll recognize it if it's related to what we found on the PCs today."

"I'll walk you out, Kate." Albert stood up. "Mr. Mendoza, do you want me here or in the IS control center tomorrow?"

"Report back here tomorrow, Albert. I appreciate your help. Both of you, have a good evening."

"Yes, sir. You, too." Kate led the way to the elevator.

Albert put his hand in front of the elevator door and let Kate get in first. "I'm starved. Do you want to grab a bite to eat?"

"Thanks anyway, but my brother is waiting for me."

Albert looked at lights indicating which floor the elevator had reached. "Maybe some other time then."

Kate also turned her attention to the descending floor numbers. "Sure. Maybe another time."

The commute out to Buckhead proved arduous indeed. Officers from the Atlanta Police Department directed traffic at major intersections. All other intersections she drove through had temporary four-way stop signs.

She finally arrived at her brother's large house in the upscale neighborhood. She knocked on the door.

Her niece answered the door with a fistful of money. "Oh, hey, Aunt Kate."

"Hi, Vicky. You don't have to pay me to come over."

The thin, pretty teenage girl glanced down at the cash in her hand. "We called for a pizza an hour and a half ago. Dad says everyone is ordering pizza so they can watch all the special coverage on the news about the hacking stuff going on."

Kate stepped past her niece. "Where is Terry?"

"Watching the news." Victoria closed the door and followed Kate inside. "You look great. Did you lose more weight?"

"About ten pounds total."

"What's his name?"

"Whose?"

"The reason you lost all that weight."

"Renato." Kate trailed behind her niece down the stairs and into the den.

"Oooh, sounds exotic. That's the guy you're trying to look good for?"

"No." She laughed. "Renato is my Jiu-Jitsu instructor. He's the reason I lost the weight. But it's from training. There's no guy."

"If you say so." Vicky rolled her eyes and plopped down on the couch next to her dad.

"What's that supposed to mean?" Kate crossed her arms.

"There's always a guy." Vicky winked.

"Have you been spreading rumors?" Kate

quizzed her brother who seemed engrossed by the news coverage.

"Nope. My lips are sealed." Terry held the remote territorially in his hand. He didn't look up until a commercial break. Then, he turned to Kate who'd taken a seat on the recliner. "What's the latest at work?"

Kate told him everything she knew so far, including her suspicions about Sky National Bank's network being infected.

"I thought you said the breach was external." Terry sat forward on the couch.

"The hacked customer PCs were external exploits, but the infiltrators got their emails from somewhere. These guys were good. If they broke into our system, there's no way they left without injecting malicious code."

Victoria sat with her legs crossed on the couch. "So these guys stole a few million, shut down the trains in DC, hacked some red lights, and turned off New York's 911 service. It doesn't really seem like that big of a deal. New York already has their emergency call system back online."

"It's a pretty big deal. If criminals knew people couldn't call the police, just think of how emboldened they'd be to do bad stuff. But in Sky National's case at least, every one of the compromised PCs had a unique bug. It's not just one virus somebody can write a patch for. It's literally like a swarm of locusts. You have to kill every one of them individually. That attack represents capabilities no one has ever seen before. I don't know that New York and DC are connected, but if they are, the situation is even worse."

"Can't you just spray locusts with bug spray?" Vicky shrugged.

"Yeah, the cyber version of that would be turning off the internet," Kate answered. "We'd go back to the 1800s."

"Would that be so bad?" Vicky inquired.

"Gas deliveries, grocery stores, banks, credit card companies, planes, trains, and electricity function with or are controlled via the internet. We don't have the infrastructure from the 1800s. So we might not last too long without it." Kate's expression was grim.

The doorbell rang. "That must be the pizza finally. I'll go get it." Vicky seemed more concerned about the attacks than she had been moments earlier.

Terry watched his daughter go up the stairs. "That's a fairly gruesome prognosis you just gave. Were you just trying to scare some sense into Vicky?"

"No. I think this is bad."

Terry motioned to the television. "They seem to have fixed the worst of it."

"For now. We don't know anything about these bugs. This could have been a test run. Think about it. The attack proved they have access to critical infrastructure and the banking system. The hackers could literally hold America hostage."

Terry leaned back on the couch. "Fortunately, we have the world reserve currency and we can print our own money, so the US is capable of paying whatever ransom they ask for."

"Unless it's an enemy country or terrorist organization who is more interested in our absolute demise than our money." Kate twisted her mouth to one side nervously.

"What are you thinking?" Terry asked.

"I don't know." Kate shook her head. "Gavin said he was going to stock up on some extra food and take his money out of the bank."

"That sounds extreme."

Kate sighed. "That's what I said. He pointed out the fact that if he's wrong, he could put his money back in after the smoke clears. He said he'd eat the food anyway."

Terry tapped his lip with his index figure pensively. "His obvious implication is that if we're wrong, we'll have no such opportunity to rectify our misjudgment."

"Yeah." Kate bit her thumbnail. "What do you think?"

"I don't know." Terry thought quietly for a while.

Vicky came bounding down the stairs with the pizza box, some paper plates, and canned sodas. "I brought you a Coke, Aunt Kate."

"Thank you." Kate placed coasters on the coffee table.

Terry placed a slice of pizza on a paper plate and passed it to his sister. "Kate, why don't you pack a bag with a couple weeks' worth of clothes and keep it over here. I'll stock up on a few extra canned goods."

Vicky chewed quickly and washed down her food with a gulp of soda. "What did I miss?"

Terry shook his head dismissively. "Nothing. Just if this hacking thing continues, Kate might feel more comfortable staying with us for a few days."

Kate held the plate and stared blankly at the lukewarm pizza. "Sure, thanks."

"What are your thoughts?" Terry bit into his slice.

She looked up slowly. "Maybe we should take some things up to the cabin."

"What? Are you serious?" Vicky spoke with a mouthful of food, veiling it only slightly with the back of her hand. "I've spent more than my share of Thanksgivings in that place and have to spend every Christmas break up there. Why would you want to go to grandpa's musty old cabin?"

"It's not musty." Terry scowled.

"Waynesville has a low population density," Kate said. "People act crazy enough as it is. If they start losing stuff because of a wide-spread computer hack, things could get hectic; especially around a city as big as Atlanta."

Vicky put her plate on the coffee table. "No way. Mom will never go for it." She spun around and looked at her dad. "Where did you say this hacker guy lives?"

Terry shot her a look that said *Shut up*.

"Charlotte, right?" Vicky snapped her fingers at Kate. "Waynesville is closer to him than Atlanta."

Kate glared at Terry. "What is she talking about?"

"Come on, don't act like you don't know." Vicky tilted her head to one side.

"You are officially out of the circle of

confidence." Terry glared at Victoria and made a circular motion with his hands. "The circle is now closed. We're inside the circle, and you're outside the circle."

Vicky waved her hands. "Whatever. If it means leaving my friends and going to the woods, I don't want to be in your crummy old circle anyway." She looked back at Kate. "You're so pretty, Aunt Kate. I mean it. And Atlanta is full of guys."

"Really, Victoria, this has nothing to do with a guy. I wouldn't drag you off to the wilderness just so I could have an excuse to be near a guy. I can't believe you think that about me."

Vicky looked at her plate remorsefully. "I'm sorry. But I have friends at school that I'd like to be near."

"Yeah, I heard."

"You heard what?" Vicky snapped her head around.

"That you've got guys calling the house."

Vicky pointed at her father. "*You* are out of the circle of confidence!" She spun her finger in a circle around her head. "The council has spoken, the circle is closed, please leave the island now."

Terry fought a grin and looked at Kate as if he were pleading for empathy. "See what I'm going to have to go through?"

Vicky resumed eating her pizza. "What about Uncle Boyd? Are you going to invite him to the cabin?"

Terry clinched his jaw and looked at Kate. "I can't imagine he'd want to come."

"Oh, if the world is falling apart, you don't think

he'd want to hide out with us?" Vicky gave her father a stern look.

Terry answered bluntly. "Uncle Boyd gets drunk and breaks stuff. He's not the best company to have around if resources are stretched thin."

"But he's your brother. He's family, Dad. You can't just abandon him." Vicky looked to Kate for support.

Kate lifted her shoulders. "He's our brother, but your dad has to do what he thinks is best for his family. He's responsible for you, Sam, and your mom. Boyd is responsible for himself. Part of being responsible is not doing things and saying stuff to your family that makes them not want to be around you."

"You're turning your back on him, too?" Vicky crossed her arms. "Grandpa left that cabin to all three of you."

Terry commented, "And Boyd wanted to sell it so he could go on a drinking tour of Europe. I bought Boyd out so the rest of us could enjoy the cabin and Uncle Boyd could go drinking."

"I hope Sam never abandons me like that." Vicky puckered her brow.

Terry tightened his lips. "If you threaten the peace of Sam's family by getting drunk at every holiday gathering and saying horrible things to his spouse, I hope he does. Family will always be family, but sometimes you have to quarantine the cancerous elements to protect the integrity of the healthy relationships."

Vicky grabbed her plate and stomped off toward the stairs. "It doesn't matter. Mom will never agree to run off to the woods anyway."

Kate waited for the cauldron of teenage angst to leave the room then looked kindly at her brother. "I certainly don't want to make trouble between you and Penny. Do whatever you think is best. I should get going."

Terry stood to hug Kate. "Bring a bag over for now, and I'll pick up a few extra dry goods tomorrow. We'll stick a pin in the idea about taking supplies to the cabin. Let me know if you find any bugs in the system at work."

CHAPTER 7

Yea, they made their hearts as an adamant stone, lest they should hear the law, and the words which the Lord of hosts hath sent in his spirit by the former prophets: therefore came a great wrath from the Lord of hosts. Therefore it is come to pass, that as he cried, and they would not hear; so they cried, and I would not hear, saith the Lord of hosts.

Zechariah 7:12-13

Kate removed her glasses and rubbed her eyes. She'd been staring at the computer screen since 6:30 Thursday morning. She glanced at her watch. "One o'clock. I've gotta get some lunch."

"Sure, go ahead," Mendoza said from his desk.

"Mind if I come along?" Albert invited himself.

Kate put her glasses back on. "Sure. Why not." She glanced back at the screen while she collected her purse and phone.

Albert walked over to her chair. "Do you want to go to Oak Wood?"

"Sure." Kate studied one last line of code.

"Mr. Mendoza, would you like us to bring you anything?" Albert offered.

"Hang on." Kate put a finger in the air. "Albert, what does that look like to you?"

Albert looked at her screen. "It looks like an alien language. I wrote code for six years prior to working here. I'm something of a digital polyglot when it comes to computer languages. In addition to SQL, I know C, C++, PHP, Python, and Java, but I've never seen anything that looks quite like that."

Mendoza walked over to look at Kate's monitor. "It's strangely familiar, yet altogether different."

Kate studied the line longer. "At first glance, it looks like SQL, enough so that it doesn't stick out like a sore thumb, but when you look closer it's nothing like any SQL code I've ever seen."

"The bugs you found on the PCs, were they written in traditional C++?" Mendoza looked at her.

"It was an odd variant of C++, but I would still call it C++," she replied.

"Like Go?" Albert asked.

"No. Not exactly like Go either," Kate clarified.

Mendoza rubbed his chin. "You think an AI program could have generated the code on the PCs. Do you think the same program could have written this?"

Kate stared at the lines of letters, symbols, and numbers. "Yeah, I do."

"What do you think this code does?" Mendoza gazed at the characters.

"Something bad. We should extract it immediately," Albert said.

"I'm not so sure about that," Kate said. "We should prep a sandbox in an offline machine and run the code to see if we can figure out what it's trying to do."

"What if this thing is getting ready to transfer all the bank's money to Russia?" Albert asked.

"Then we better skip lunch and order Chinese." Kate copied the code to a document file and printed it out.

Two hours later, Kate peered at the fourth computer, which Mendoza had brought in to use as a sandbox for the virus. "It's essentially a logic bomb. But whatever the command is, it's only designed to send a signal to another program. I'm guessing that it functions like a dead-man switch. If we try to remove this line of code, we'll probably trigger some other command. If we take the entire system offline that will also trigger it."

"But we have no idea what that command is?" Mendoza looked over her shoulder.

"I may have just found the other program. Look at this, it's a massive block of code. We're talking ten times bigger than Stuxnet." Albert looked up from his computer.

Kate and Mr. Mendoza quickly walked over to Albert's workstation.

"Where did you find that?" Kate asked.

"I was searching through HR's applications. They keep tons of resumes scanned as PDFs. This was nestled inside them. It's an EXE file but was masquerading as a PDF. The really bad news is that it's running right now."

Kate looked at Mr. Mendoza. "We have to take our network down right now."

"You said that could trigger the logic bomb." His face looked stressed.

"Yeah, but whatever this thing is designed to do is already happening. We don't know what this program is capable of. This could be the cyber version of a nuclear bomb. We have to shut it down before it infects anything else," she pleaded.

"Maybe we could pull the plug but connect the network to a false internet connection to trick the logic bomb into thinking we're still online." Albert turned to Kate.

"Could that work?" Mendoza asked.

She frowned. "Theoretically, yes. But I'm not sure the program would fall for it. We could loop internet traffic, like looping a few seconds of security footage so a security guard doesn't know his camera is down. It's a gamble. We're basically betting on the virus being a lazy, complacent security guard."

"What are the odds of that?" Mendoza inquired.

"Given the complexity of this code?" Kate nervously twisted her mouth. "Slim."

"I'm going to call Xavier. I think it's time we alerted the authorities." Mendoza pulled out his phone and walked toward the hall.

Kate, Albert, and Zachery Mendoza worked frantically looking for more malicious code while they waited for an agent from the FBI's Cyber Division. Soon, the speakerphone on Mr. Mendoza's desk sprang to life. "Mr. Mendoza, Agent Ulasen is here to see you."

"Thank you, Janet. Send him in." Mendoza stood to receive his guest.

Ulasen was young, early thirties, Kate guessed. He was thin and looked more like someone from DefCon than an FBI agent.

Mr. Mendoza made introductions and explained what the team knew so far.

Ulasen looked over the massive piece of code which Albert had identified. He shook his head. "What is that? It's not C, it's not C++, and it certainly isn't Go."

Kate felt relieved to not have an agent who was completely in the dark about what he was looking at. "We believe it's some derivative language that is compatible with other object-oriented languages."

"Who wrote it?"

"We think it could have been written by an AI program." Kate watched the agent.

"How would the other programs understand this code if it's not in a recognizable language?" He looked perplexed.

Albert answered, "It could still issue commands in C or C++. It's just here to inflict damage. It doesn't need for the other programs to be fluent in whatever this babel is. Kind of like if you went to Mexico to buy drugs or weapons. If you had a pocket full of cash and knew a few keywords, you could accomplish your mission without having a perfect command of the Spanish language."

Agent Ulasen glared at Albert as if he thought that was a very peculiar choice of analogies. "Drugs or weapons?"

Kate immediately stepped in. She pointed at the empty Chinese food containers. "Or Kung Pao Chicken; none of us are fluent in Mandarin, and the folks at the restaurant have broken English at best, but we can still make specific transactions."

"I suppose so." Ulasen turned away from Albert and seemed to dismiss the ill-conceived metaphor. "Given the recent string of activity, I'm going to call in someone from NSA to advise us on how to proceed. I don't feel comfortable taking your network offline."

"How long do you think that will be? This thing could be infecting other computers. These are all zero-day exploits. Our network is communicating with every other bank in America, all the major credit card companies, the Federal Reserve, and the SWIFT system." Albert sounded pushy and demanding.

Kate's issue was social anxiety, which caused her to be extremely reticent around people she wasn't familiar with. Albert Rogers, however, seemed to lack any sense of reservation whatsoever and was liable to say anything, to anyone, at any time, regardless of whether he was acquainted with the individual or not.

Ulasen seemed perturbed by Albert's petulant outburst. "I'm sure they'll have someone here within the hour, Mr. Rogers. We are well aware of the threat we're dealing with here."

Mendoza shot Albert a gruff look then turned to the FBI agent. "Can I have Janet get you a bottled water or a cup of coffee?"

"Coffee would be fine," said Ulasen.

When the team from NSA rolled in, it couldn't have been more different from Agent Ulasen's arrival. Ten agents came into the room as if they were performing a no-knock raid. Kate, Albert, and Mr. Mendoza were all separated like they were suspects in a major terrorist plot.

Two agents escorted Kate to a separate room where she was aggressively debriefed. One of the agents acted as the liaison and the other was obviously from the tech side of the operation.

"When did you first recognize anything suspicious? Why didn't you notify the authorities immediately when you suspected you had an infection? How long have you been working with the bank?" The big, intimidating NSA agent fired out question after question to Kate. This treatment immediately caused her to have a panic attack and she clammed up, almost unable to speak.

"I . . . I . . . I . . . don't know. You're frightening me!"

"This is a serious situation. That's a normal response. But you need to tell me everything you know."

She shook her head, nearly paralyzed by anxiety. "Everything is on my computer. I don't know what it is. I just know the code isn't supposed to be there."

The tech looked on at Kate, as if he felt sorry for her. "Larry, why don't you get her a bottle of water and give her a chance to calm down. She looks a little rattled."

Larry grunted and started to go out the door. He spun around before leaving. "Give me your cell phone."

She handed it over without a fight.

Larry stuck it in his pocket and handed her a plain white envelope.

"What's this?" she asked skittishly.

"It's a National Security Letter. Basically a gag order. You can't discuss anything you've seen in the past two days. Not even with the people who helped you identify the code."

"Okay, I won't. But how are we supposed to fix it?"

"Don't worry about that. We'll take it from here." Larry began to walk out but turned around again. "Oh, and I need the names and telephone numbers of everyone you've told about this situation. And don't try to lie to me thinking you're saving them from getting in trouble. I have your phone and I'm going to dump all of your communications from the last two days."

Kate felt horrific, like she'd committed high treason.

Larry finally left.

"I'm Oscar. Don't let him bother you. You're not in any trouble."

Kate wondered if it was some kind of good-cop-bad-cop routine. In the end, she didn't care. She was simply happy to have someone who wasn't barking at her like a rabid dog.

"I'm with Tailored Access Operations. Have you heard of my department?"

She avoided direct eye contact. "You guys developed EternalBlue and DoublePulsar."

He crossed his hands. "I wish I could answer that, but I'm sure you wouldn't be surprised if I told you I can't."

She expected nothing different.

Oscar spoke softly. "What can you tell me about what you found on the bank's network?"

She explained that they'd discovered two pieces of code. She minimized the details, still feeling like she was in trouble for something.

"What languages were they written in?"

Kate immediately recognized that Oscar was digging. Why would he think to ask such a specific question? She shrugged. "Um, it looked like SQL on the mainframe but I didn't recognize the functions. The one in the HR files was either C or C++."

"You don't know the difference?"

"I do, but again, the code wasn't anything I'm familiar with."

"Agent Ulasen said one of you speculated that the language seemed abnormally foreign; as if it might have been written by artificial intelligence."

She shook her head. "I've never seen code written by AI, so I wouldn't know."

Oscar said politely, "Okay. If you can just write down those names and numbers for Larry, you can go on home for the day. You guys did good work finding the code. But make sure you keep it to yourself. We don't want to start a panic."

"Absolutely." Kate pulled the National Security Letter out of the envelope and began writing down the names of the people she'd talked to on the manilla paper. "Agent . . . Larry has my phone. I'll need it to get the numbers."

"Of course. He should be back with that in a moment." Oscar smiled benignly.

CHAPTER 8

That they may know from the rising of the sun to its setting that there is none besides Me. I am the Lord, and there is no other; I form the light and create darkness, I make peace and create calamity; I, the Lord, do all these things.

Isaiah 45:6-7 NKJV

At her home Thursday evening, Kate looked despairingly at the two empty pint containers of midnight-cookies-and-cream ice cream. She gripped her phone, feeling worse than horrible about what she had to do next. The only possible thing more dreadful than telling her brother how she'd given his information to the NSA was not telling him.

She knew Terry would understand. But what about Vijay, Shu, and Willow? Yet more than any of them, she worried about how Gavin would feel about it.

"Best get this over with," she said aloud. Kate sent a text to Terry. *NSA stopped by today. Wanted to know who else knew about what was going on at work. They dumped my phone so I had to tell them. Long story short, I'm not allowed to talk about it. Don't be surprised if they come see you.*

She sighed, then duplicated the communication to Vijay, Shu, and Willow via the Wire app.

Terry texted her back. *Are you home?*

Yes. She typed her reply.

I'll come over after dinner.

OK. Kate looked up from her phone and exhaled.

A message came in from Vijay. *No worries.*

Shu was next to reply. *Thanks for the heads up.*

Shortly thereafter, Willow's reply simply said, *Not your fault.*

Kate anxiously messaged Gavin through the Wire app. Then, she waited. She fidgeted with her hair, staring at the screen but no reply came. After thirty minutes of nothing, she got up from the couch. She collected the empty ice cream containers and took them to the trash. She checked the freezer to make sure she didn't have a third pint stashed behind a stack of frozen vegetables.

Her heart jumped when she heard a knock at the door. She checked the peephole before turning the deadbolt and removing the chain.

Terry walked in. He looked around her apartment. "Are we alone?"

She glanced at her phone. "Not really; we live in an Orwellian surveillance state. Big brother is always listening."

He pressed his lips together tightly.

"Did anyone come see you?" Kate asked.

"Not yet, but I saw some of them in the elevator before I left the office. It's like an invasion." He looked around again, as if he thought he might be able to spot a poorly-disguised microphone planted at the base of one of Kate's lamps or in an air vent. "Why don't we go get something to eat." He nodded at her phone. "We can leave our tracking devices in the car."

Kate wanted to talk to him about everything. She needed to vent and welcomed the idea of getting away from anything the NSA might be using to eavesdrop on her. "Sure."

She followed Terry out the door and to the elevator. Kate continued to check her phone for a reply from Gavin on the way to the restaurant. It would be sheer torture if he didn't respond before she went inside and she had to abandon her phone. Still, no message came.

Terry drove to the restaurant and said nothing on the way. Once he'd parked and the two of them were out of the car, he asked, "Is everything okay? You look distressed."

"The visit had me shook up, but I've calmed down from that. I notified Gavin of the visit. He hasn't messaged me back. I think he's mad at me for telling the NSA that he knows about the breach."

"I'm sure he'll contact you. Give it time." Terry

chose a seat near the window and slid into the booth opposite of Kate.

Kate scanned the room to make sure they hadn't been followed. Once they placed their order, she quickly explained to Terry what had happened at work.

"Wow. A National Security Letter. That's serious."

"Yeah. You might have your own copy soon. I will say it's high-quality paper with an embossed seal on the letterhead. Were it not for the nature of the communique, it would be suitable for framing."

Terry forced a smile. "So what are you thinking?"

"I think all of this is a result of some highly-sophisticated cyber weapon that they lost control of. But, I think the genie is out of the bottle and they know they'll never get it back inside."

"Hmm." Terry stared pensively at his ice tea.

"It's a time bomb, Terry. We need to be ready when it goes off."

He interlaced his fingers. "What do you want to do?"

"I want to make a run up to Waynesville and stock up the cabin."

"Are you going to take stuff with you or are you going to buy it there?"

She shook her head. "I haven't given it that much thought yet. I suppose I'll take my old clothes; things I don't wear anymore. But they have a Walmart and plenty of grocery stores. I guess I'll buy the other supplies when I get there. It might be more than I can haul in one trip anyway."

"How much stuff are you going to buy?"

"I don't know. A few months' worth maybe. I don't even know what a month's worth of food looks like."

"Would this be a project you could take on yourself? Out of an abundance of caution, I took a few thousand dollars out of the bank. I can give you some money to stock up food for us."

"I can do that."

"When do you think you'll go?"

"Seems the NSA doesn't want me around the office. I guess I'll go first thing in the morning. Who knows how long we have until this thing blows up."

"You'll come back to Atlanta, right?"

"If nothing happens by the time I have to go back to work, I guess I will. But that's a big *if*."

Terry pulled a white bank envelope out of his back pocket. He extracted a stack of one-hundred-dollar bills and counted them out. "Will five thousand be enough?" He passed the pile of bills across the table.

"I would imagine that will buy a lot of canned goods." She took the money.

She looked from side to side. "The NSA already made me feel like a terrorist. Now I feel like a drug dealer, too."

The food arrived and the two discussed what types of items might come in handy if a widespread cyber-attack were to incapacitate the country's most basic services.

Afterward, Terry paid the check and the siblings exited the restaurant. Terry held the door open for

Kate. "Are you going to tell Boyd?"

She huffed. "I can't talk to anyone about any of this, remember?"

"Yeah, but you could pose it as it just being us taking precautions because of the attacks this week. You wouldn't be disclosing anything that hasn't been all over the news."

"You want me to tell him?"

Terry sighed. "He's more likely to listen to you than me."

"I'll say something to him. I'll give him a call on the way up tomorrow. But I doubt he'll pay any attention to me. Even if I could tell him everything he wouldn't take it seriously. There's no way he'll want to act based on a few temporary service outages."

"But our hands will be clean." Terry opened the door of his Mercedes.

Kate got in the passenger's side. "If anything happens and he knows we're stocked with supplies, you know he'll show up after the fact."

Terry bit his lip. He pulled the envelope back out and counted off more bills. "Here's an extra thousand. Stock up for him, too."

Kate stuffed the cash in her purse. She powered on her phone. She had a notification of a new Wire message. She hesitated before opening it. Sure enough, it was from Gavin.

G-men came by. Couldn't talk. Check your spam.

Kate figured she'd received an encrypted communication via email. She also knew the NSA was watching her and couldn't be sure what types of surveillance tools they were running on her phone. Rather than risking it, she waited until she got home.

Terry pulled up near the front door of Kate's apartment building. "Do you want to come out to the house? You could stay with us tonight. You might sleep better."

She wanted to get in contact with Gavin. "No thanks. I'll be fine. I want to get an early start tomorrow. If I get to the cabin by lunch, I can make a few runs to the store before evening."

"Okay. Be safe and drive carefully."

She exited the vehicle. "I will."

Once inside her apartment, she pulled out an old laptop which she'd refurbished with a fresh hard drive and memory stick as a project machine. She powered up the computer and booted the TAILS operating system, which left no trace of any online activities. Next, she opened a TOR browser and then opened her email. She checked her spam folder.

She read the first subject line out loud. "Work from home to earn extra income and fast cash 100% free program in Charlotte." Kate laughed. "Every word in the subject line except *Charlotte* flagged this message as spam. He's over the top."

She read the name of the sender. "Get rich quick scam at Gmail.com." Right away, she knew Gavin would never use Gmail for the actual communication. She figured another email address had to be hidden in the message.

Once opened, the email had a lame photoshopped image of a guy on a beach with a computer and stacks of cash. The email had no text.

Kate downloaded the image then read the name of the image file. "NC hacker boy at Proton."

"I got you." Kate quickly went to ProtonMail and opened a new account. "How about GA hacker girl?" She quickly entered a password and composed an email. *Got your message.*

She entered Gavin's secret ProtonMail address and sent the correspondence.

Seconds later, a notification popped up in her inbox. She opened the email. *We need to talk.*

It's not safe, she replied.

The next message contained only a frowny face emoji.

She did something she never did, she took a chance. Kate typed back, *Going to your state tomorrow.*

How far from me? Gavin inquired.

She paused before typing in the answer. She didn't want it to be obvious that she'd already done the math on the distance between Charlotte and Waynesville. *Looks like about two and a half hours.*

Could we meet for lunch?

Excitement bubbled up inside her like a warm root beer. She replied, *Sweet Onion.* It had been her father's favorite restaurant in Waynesville. Other than revealing the name of the restaurant, she'd taken every precaution and still said nothing that would get her in trouble with the NSA. Still, she'd say nothing of the hack until they finished eating. Then, they'd stash their phones in the car and go for a walk to discuss the forbidden topic.

CHAPTER 9

The Lord is good, a strong hold in the day of trouble; and he knoweth them that trust in him. But with an overrunning flood he will make an utter end of the place thereof, and darkness shall pursue his enemies.

Nahum 1:7-8

Late Friday morning, Kate drove up the steep gravel driveway to the rustic log cabin. The old home always evoked feelings of nostalgia. Kate remembered going there with her family as a child. Terry had made sure the cabin was meticulously maintained. He'd put a metal roof on it three years earlier and paid to have the exterior re-stained every five years like clockwork. Kate always offered to chip in, but Terry would never accept her money.

At 3,000 feet above sea level, the late September air was much cooler than it had been in Atlanta. With her backpack over her shoulder, Kate climbed the familiar wooden staircase to the front porch and unlocked the front door. The initial smell inside was a touch musty, but like the flavors in a complex wine, it held many other distinct fragrances. Notes of strong coffee, charred wood, and comfortable quilts mingled with the stale aroma. Kate dropped her pack by the door and went through the cabin, opening all the windows so it could air out. She looked around for a while, allowing a few moments for sentiments before hauling her pack upstairs to her room. She tossed the bag on her bed, checked the time, and went into the bathroom to freshen up.

"Don't act like a dork," she told the girl in the mirror. "Or a stalker." Kate brushed mascara through her lashes, checked her teeth, and turned out the light. She descended the stairs with enthusiasm, locked the door behind her, and made her way to the car.

She arrived at the restaurant shortly after noon. She walked inside and scanned the tables for a single guy. She didn't see Gavin anywhere.

"Kate?"

She turned around to see him right behind her. "Hey. You made it."

"Yeah, I should have thought to ask what time you eat lunch. I've been here since eleven."

"Oh, sorry to keep you waiting. Did you eat already?"

"No. I've been at the bar, hassling the

bartender."

"For an hour? You're not sloshed, are you?"

He chuckled. "No. I had one cream soda. I rarely drink, and certainly not at eleven o'clock."

"Table for two?" The hostess picked up some menus from the stand.

"Yes, please," Gavin answered and trailed behind the hostess.

Kate followed Gavin. Once they were seated, she asked, "Did you leave your phone in the car?"

"Yeah. You?"

"Yep."

Gavin looked at her silently for a while. "You look great."

"Thanks." She turned away bashfully.

He picked up his menu. "So, the boys from Fort Mead came to see you, too?"

"Yeah, but I'd rather talk about it after lunch."

"Don't want it to spoil your appetite?"

She looked around. "I don't want to take the chance that they bugged the restaurant."

Gavin seemed to be fighting a grin. "Wow! They've really got you spooked. I think they have about all they can handle right now. I seriously doubt they have the resources to hack an encrypted email dialogue between two unknown parties and send out a team to bug the whole restaurant.

"If they possessed a billionth of the competence you give them credit for, this thing never would have happened in the first place."

She looked around once more, considered Gavin's logic, then said very softly. "So you think the locusts are a product of the NSA."

He casually studied the menu. "I think they are a product of a product of the NSA, yes. The way those guys were acting yesterday, they know something. They didn't seem a bit surprised by anything I told them. We found four zero-day exploits in four machines. I don't care who you are, information like that should raise an eyebrow."

"Are they looking through your servers at the bank?"

"Yep. Sent us all home. Like something out of E.T. or Close Encounters where the government quarantines the site of an alien landing. What about you?"

"Same thing."

"So, what brings you to my fair state?"

"My dad left us a cabin up here. I thought I'd buy a few things. You know, stock the pantry. I figured it will be a good place for me and my brother's family to lay low if things get hectic."

"I guess you found something in your network."

"What makes you say that?"

Gavin dropped his menu on the table and looked her in the eyes. "You thought I was overreacting two days ago when I mentioned buying a few extra items from the grocery and taking some money out of the bank. Now you're literally heading for the hills."

"I'm not heading for the hills. I'm just being prudent. What you said made sense. I was wrong to say you overreacted."

"Hmm."

The waitress approached the table. "What can I get for you folks?"

He picked up his menu again. "Kate?"

"I'll have the trout."

Gavin perked up. "In that case, may I please order the bacon-wrapped meatloaf?"

"Sure. It will be out shortly." The waitress took the menus.

"Why did you say, *in that case*?"

"You ordered the fish, which at least means you're not a vegan. Lots of girls in the tech space think they have to eat like they live in Silicon Valley."

"If I were a vegan, you would have ordered a vegetarian meal?"

"I don't know about vegetarian, but bacon-wrapped meatloaf is almost the antithesis of everything a vegan stands for. But, considering it's you, yeah, I probably would have ordered a salad."

"Why? What do I have to do with it?"

"Oh, come on. You were the hottest chick at DefCon."

She blushed and looked away. Kate sincerely hoped he wasn't toying with her. "Stop it! That's not even close to true and you know it. What about all the girls in the little shorts and the outfits hocking the latest antivirus software?"

He put his hands up. "Okay, I'll meet you halfway. You were the hottest girl at DefCon who wasn't *paid* to be there."

Still, that was a very high compliment. One Kate did not feel herself to be worthy of. "If you're not just kidding around, then thank you."

Gavin interlaced his fingers and put his hands on the table. "Are you going to make me beg?"

"I have no idea what you're talking about."

"What did you find on your machines?"

She pressed her lips together tightly.

He said, "You've already violated the NSL. If this was some elaborate sting operation, you'd already be on your way to a CIA black site. In for a penny, in for a pound."

She whispered, "The network had multiple instances of malicious code."

"Okay, that's vague, but it's a good starting point."

"One seemed to be a logic bomb, a triggering device for other viruses. The other one was more complex than anything I've ever seen."

"You have a copy of the Stuxnet source code, right?"

"Yeah. This was exponentially more elaborate. And it wasn't even written in a standardized language." She continued to provide more details about what she, Albert, and Mendoza had discovered.

Gavin listened keenly.

Lunch arrived and the two spent the next hour talking about the intricacies of the multiple pieces of new malware that had emerged over the past week.

Afterward, the two exited the restaurant.

"Are you in a hurry? Do you have time to walk around and see if we can spot a good place for dessert?" Gavin asked.

"Yeah, I could hang out for another hour or so, but I do have a mission to complete."

"I understand. Don't let me keep you from doing

what you need to do." He looked slightly disappointed.

Kate wondered if the good looking, dark-haired, guy who actually liked the same things she liked might actually be interested. She'd had guys flirt with her before who weren't really interested. She wasn't good at reading between the lines when it came to guys and didn't want to deal with the disappointment if Gavin wasn't genuinely attracted to her. Still, she didn't want to frighten him off if he was. "You're welcome to tag along if you want. I'll just be wagging groceries up the hill to the cabin. Kinda boring."

"I'd be happy to give you a hand. Sounds like it might be a chore that would go faster if you had some help."

"Okay." She smiled. "Then at least let me buy dessert, as a thank you."

"Deal. I need to stop by my vehicle and check my phone. I want to make sure work isn't trying to reach me."

"Where did you park?"

"In the public lot across the street."

"There's plenty of open spaces in front of the restaurant."

"Yeah, but I wanted to make sure I wasn't being tailed."

"And you accused me of being paranoid. What about that big speech you gave me about the NSA not having resources?"

"Oh, they could hire a PI or a private contractor to tail me. The government prints their own money. It literally costs them nothing. Cash is not a limited resource for them. But everything else I said still stands."

"Whatever." Kate looked around at the beautiful mountains that laced the horizon in every direction.

"What are you thinking of buying? Just food and stuff, or are you going all-out survivalist?"

"I wouldn't know where to begin for all-out survival. I'll buy some canned goods and hope it isn't too bad."

"That's better than nothing. I don't really know what else to do either."

Kate paused when she reached the street. "What's that place, with the red awning?"

"Beats me. You know more about this town than I do."

"Yeah, but I've never noticed that store before. Carolina Readiness Supply. What kind of readiness do you suppose they specialize in?"

"Maybe readiness for a massive computer virus that's about to end the world as we know it. Only one way to find out." Gavin seemed to have dismissed his concerns about whether his job had tried to contact him and walked briskly toward the glass storefront beneath the red awning.

Kate quickened her pace to keep up. She read the signage aloud as they approached the store. "Solar generators, heirloom seeds, first aid kits, water purifiers, sounds like these folks have been thinking about *what if* for a long time."

"Sounds like we might need a few more items than just some canned goods." Gavin held the door open for Kate.

She stepped through the door and spent a few

moments just looking around.

"Can I help you?" A gentleman asked.

"Uh, yeah. Maybe so." She didn't know where to begin.

CHAPTER 10

A prudent man foreseeth the evil, and hideth himself: but the simple pass on, and are punished.

Proverbs 22:3

Kate examined a selection of water filters hanging on a rack. "What type of readiness, exactly, does your store specialize in? I mean, is there a specific event that people who shop here are preparing for?"

"I'm Bill." He offered a warm handshake.

"Nice to meet you. I'm Kate, and this is Gavin."

"Folks who come in here are typically concerned about a variety of possible disasters. Economic collapse, EMP attack, civil war, pandemics." Bill chuckled. "I even get a few people now and again getting ready for the zombie apocalypse. I don't think most of them are serious. It's probably just funny to show their friends that they have a gas mask and a machete. But who knows, maybe some of them believe in it. I'm not judging. Plenty of folks laugh at us for prepping."

Kate picked up a small USB solar charger. "I see. Let's say someone was concerned about social unrest, maybe due to a system's failure in the banking industry. What types of items might you recommend?"

Bill walked closer. "Every event has its own small set of special preparations, but ninety-nine percent of it is the same, whether you're talking about an EMP, the zombie apocalypse, or a failure of the banking system. When you say system's failure, are you talking about a bank holiday like they had in Cyprus a few years back, or do you mean a cyber-attack?"

Kate was hesitant to get more specific. "Either one I guess. Just hypothetically."

Bill didn't press her. "For both of those scenarios, it makes sense to keep some cash outside of the banking system. Of course, that's true for an EMP, pandemic, or most any other threat. If you have significant assets, you might want to think about converting a portion of your cash into gold and silver. Dollars will be king for the first few days of a collapse, but that party won't last long."

A woman walked into the back door. "Hi."

Bill introduced her. "This is my wife, Jan."

"Hi," Gavin said. "Are you two . . ?"

"Preppers?" Jan finished his sentence.

"Yeah, I guess, if that's not an offensive word or anything," said Gavin.

She replied, "I've been called worse. But to answer your question, yes, we believe in being ready for whatever."

Bill put his arm around her and pulled her close. "We practice what we preach."

Kate moved over to the shelves stocked with plastic buckets full of long-term survival food. "What about general readiness?"

Bill said, "Think about the things you need to survive from day to day. The most basic elements are water, shelter, food, and security. If we ever have a serious crisis, starvation, dehydration, and violence will be the big killers. And when I say security, I'm not just talking about guns. Most bad stuff happens at night, so you have to be able to see in the dark. Best case scenario is to have some reliable night vision, but that can get expensive. At a bare minimum, I'd recommend some decent weapon-mounted flashlights. And communications—your security team has to be able to communicate with one another. You'll need some type of radios. We carry walkie-talkies, and we also carry hand-held Ham radios. Unless it's an emergency, you need a license to transmit with the Hams, but not to listen. Of course, a complete collapse of society would qualify as an emergency in my book.

"Now, all those electronics won't last long if you don't have rechargeable batteries and a way to recharge them. The cheapest solution is a portable solar panel and a universal battery charger, which connects to the USB in the fold-up solar panel." Bill retrieved examples of his recommendations from the shelf for Kate to inspect.

"A glitch in the banking system isn't going to affect the power." Kate studied the products.

Gavin took one of the foldable solar panels and a charger for himself. "The attacks earlier this week affected communications, emergency services, and transportation. It's hard to say whether any future attacks might disrupt electric services."

"That's true." Kate took the items from Bill. She picked up a pair of walkie-talkies and some rechargeable batteries. "My dad left us a cabin up here, over in Apple Blossom Acres. So shelter is pretty well covered."

"Our friends have a place in there. Big lots. Very nice community," Jan handed a basket to Kate.

Kate offloaded the growing pile of gear into the basket and carried it by the handle. "We're on a well, I can't imagine anything would hurt our water supply."

"Then you're on an electric pump. If the power goes out, that well won't do you much good," said Bill.

Jan walked to the next aisle and came back holding a small Sawyer water filter. "Water is such an important commodity, it wouldn't hurt to have a backup plan just in case. You can live about three days without water, but they probably won't be the best three days of your life if you're dying of dehydration."

"I'll definitely take one of these." Kate placed the filter in her basket and shifted her focus to the long-term-storage food. "How many food buckets would I need for six people?"

"Depends on how long you are planning for." Jan followed them down the aisle.

Kate couldn't even imagine how long things might go haywire if all the banks went offline. "Let's say one month for starters. I'm also going to make a few trips to the grocery and figure out how much everything costs. I'll probably be back for more."

"Okay, one month of food for six people." Jan looked at the food buckets.

Kate's eyes darted to Gavin then back at the food. She wasn't about to invite him to come survive the apocalypse with her without getting to know him better. And even if she did decide to do such a thing, she'd have to discuss it with Terry. Nevertheless, she figured it couldn't hurt to have a little extra on hand. "Better make it seven people."

"Fine," Jan responded. "Are you more concerned with value or quality?"

Kate bit her fingernail. "That's a good question. Is there a middle-of-the-road brand that you'd recommend?"

"Mountain House is good. Being so close to the Appalachian Trail, we have campers who come in here for Mountain House. It's not the apocalypse, and yet it's their first choice for a good hot meal on the trail. That speaks volumes. It's not the cheapest option, but you could offset it by taking a few of the Augason Farms buckets to bulk up the calories."

"Okay. Can you load me up with a variety of each brand?" Kate selected a few tactical flashlights and brought her merchandise up to the counter.

"Sure. If you want to pull your car up to the front door, Bill will help you load."

Gavin winked at Bill. "I'm guessing this isn't the first time you've been volunteered for such a task."

"That's very perceptive of you." Bill grinned.

Jan rang up the total and Kate paid her in cash. She was surprised at how much food she'd bought for the price. "I'll be right back." Kate sprinted across the street to retrieve her Mini and drove up to the door.

All of the supplies wouldn't fit in Kate's Mini, so Gavin brought up his Jeep Cherokee to haul the rest.

Afterward, Kate led the way to the cabin, where Gavin assisted her with unloading the stockpile into the garage beneath the house, which accounted for approximately half of the basement space.

"You can fit a lot of supplies in here. You might want to pick up some cheap shelves at one of the big-box home improvement stores if you're still planning to buy a bunch of canned goods."

"Good idea, thanks." Kate looked at the small amount of space occupied by her first haul and calculated how much room would be necessary for six months' worth of food.

"Have you thought about security? Bill said that's in the top four most important survival elements."

"My dad kept a pump-action shotgun here. Maybe I'll pick up a few more shells for it." She tucked her hands in her back jeans pockets. "What about you?"

"I have a small 9mm pistol that I keep on my

nightstand. But I'm thinking about getting something a little more serious. You only have the one shotgun for your entire family?"

"Yep, just the one. But it's pretty quiet up here. I can't imagine things would get so bad that we'd need a bunch of guns."

"I hope you're right. But, you should probably take the shotgun back to Atlanta with you. Do you know how to use it?"

"Yeah. My dad taught me to shoot when I was a teenager. It's been a while, but it'll come back to me."

"Good. You never know, it could be rough getting out of the city if everything falls apart."

She crossed her arms. "Maybe I will take it back with me. I should probably have my brother look at it and make sure it's in good working order."

Gavin looked at his Jeep. "I guess I should get going." He glanced back at Kate. "Unless you need help making a few runs to the grocery."

She wanted to ask him to hang around a little longer, but she didn't feel right making him haul her supplies if she wasn't going to invite him to come to the cabin when things got bad. It was simply too soon for that. "I'll be fine. I need to think about what I'm going to get before I go to the store anyway."

He looked a little disappointed. "Sure. Thanks for having lunch with me. Let me know the next time you come to North Carolina. Maybe we can hang out again."

"Okay, I'd like that."

His expression lifted. "Great, we'll talk soon."

"Yeah, see you soon." She watched Gavin get into his Jeep and waved.

CHAPTER 11

But if the watchman see the sword come, and blow not the trumpet, and the people be not warned; if the sword come, and take any person from among them, he is taken away in his iniquity; but his blood will I require at the watchman's hand.

Ezekiel 33:6

Sunday morning, Kate drove south on US 23. The road passed through picturesque mountain landscapes, and besides passing through a few small towns, remained very rural until it approached Atlanta. She called Terry on her way home.

"Hey, Sis. How did it go?"

"Not bad. I spent most of the money you gave

me."

"That's why I gave it to you. I appreciate you taking on the task. How much food did you get?"

"I think it's enough to last us over six months. I bought a lot of food. I had to buy shelves to put all of it on. Did you know Waynesville has a store that sells survival stuff?"

"No kidding. Did you go in?"

"Yeah, I nearly bought them out."

"I can't imagine a store like that being able to stay in business in such a small town."

"Evidently, a large percentage of the population is made up of people getting ready for one thing or the other."

"Then I suppose it will be a good place to be if things turn south."

"Yeah." Kate kept her eyes on the road while she chatted with Terry on the speaker. "Did you buy some extra food for your house?"

"I did, but not six months' worth."

"What did Penny say about it?"

"She thinks I'm overreacting. Did you call Boyd?"

"I did. He pretty much laughed it off."

"Was he sober?"

"Yeah, I called him in the middle of the day yesterday. He was at an open house. I guess being a real estate agent is the only job that offers the flexibility for Boyd to maintain his happy-go-lucky lifestyle."

"That's a polite way of putting it. It's a shame. He'd make a very successful agent if he wasn't such a lush."

"Well, people can change. You never know."

Terry said, "People change, but they usually need an extreme catalyst to motivate them. Boyd won't give up drinking until he hits bottom."

"Are you going to work tomorrow?"

"As far as I know. What about you?"

"They told me they'd let me know when they wanted us back and I haven't heard anything. I'm not planning on it at this point."

"Things seemed to have settled down in the news cycle. Maybe all of this will blow over and our worry will prove to have been in vain."

"It may blow over, they may manage to fix it, but our concern is very well merited. You know I can't say anything else about it."

"I know. I should let you go. Call me tomorrow and tell me if you go back to work."

"I will. Bye." Kate clicked off the call.

That evening she sat staring at the spiral bound notebook she'd used to write down the supplies she'd bought. She opened her laptop and began entering all the items into a spreadsheet so she could calculate the exact number of calories she'd stockpiled to see how accurate her estimate was. Her phone vibrated. She looked to see she'd received a message on her Wire app. Hoping it was a message from Gavin, she quickly swiped her screen with her finger.

The message was from Vijay. *Looks like one of your coworkers violated the NSL. Not good for him. Turn on 60 Minutes.*

Kate was perplexed by Vijay's comment, yet she

picked up the remote and navigated through the channels. When she reached the program, she felt entirely surreal. Kate watched Albert being interviewed on the familiar news magazine show. "What is he doing?"

Her question was soon answered. She listened to her colleague blow the whistle on everything that he knew. He offered up detailed commentary about the zero-day viruses that had been the real culprit of Sky National Bank's outages on the previous Tuesday. Then, he elaborated about the NSA taking over the bank's Information Security and Information Technology departments. Without mentioning names, Albert explained that many of his co-workers agreed that the viruses currently in the bank's system were a product of stolen NSA technology.

She listened closely as Albert neatly rolled up his theory to the reporter.

"I believe that at this very second, America is on the precipice of Cyber Armageddon. I've worked in the IS industry for more than a decade and I've never seen anything like this. My worst fears were confirmed when the NSA stormed into my workplace, expelled the entire Information Security team from the building, and issued National Security Letters to each and every one of us. Whatever this thing is, they are responsible for it, and they have no idea how to stop it."

The reporter asked, "Aren't you worried what the NSA will do to you for blowing the whistle and violating the NSL?"

"No. What are they going to do? Lock me up for telling the truth? The whole country knows that they're trying to keep them in the dark. The public will never stand for it."

Kate planted her face into her palm. She pleaded with the image on the television screen. "Albert! You idiot! Did the American public stand up for Edward Snowden when he told them the NSA was keeping them in the dark? Did they take to the streets for William Benny, Ed Loomis, or Thomas Drake when the government raided their homes and locked them up for outing the predecessor to Prism?" She looked back up and held out her hands. "You're smarter than this, Albert!"

Her phone rang. It was Terry.

"Hello?"

"Are you watching 60 Minutes?"

"Yeah."

"I can't believe this! This guy is going to disappear into the bowels of Hell. This is going to incite a bank run in the morning. I'm glad I took out a bunch of cash last week."

Kate thought quickly. "You could be right. Or then again, people may completely dismiss the report. Either way, I'm going to hit the ATM. I took out some money, but right now, I'm wishing I had taken more. I'll call you when I get back."

"Okay, be safe."

"See ya." She clicked off the phone, grabbed her purse and jacket, then headed out the door.

Another call came as soon as she got off the elevator. "Mr. Mendoza, hello."

"Did you know Albert was going to pull this stunt?" He sounded angry.

"I had no idea, sir. I would have begged him not to go through with it. Albert doesn't have a filter that keeps him from blurting stuff out at times, but I never thought he'd do something like this."

"If the press tries to contact you, tell them you can't talk. Neither confirm nor deny any of their questions. Don't say anything. Is that clear?"

"Crystal, sir."

"Good." Mendoza hung up.

Kate had never heard the man so upset, but then again, she'd never seen anything like Albert's interview. Once on the street, she saw no evidence of a panicked populace. Nevertheless, she carried out her mission and sprinted to the nearest ATM. She was limited to taking out $500 Sunday night. However, she'd be first in line at the teller's window on Monday morning.

The next day, Kate pulled into the nearest branch of Sky National Bank at 8:30. Five people stood lined up at the front door, waiting for it to be unlocked. "It could be worse." Kate slung her backpack over her shoulder and joined the others. The people in the line spoke to one another about Albert's revelation. She added nothing to the conversation but merely listened.

By the time the doors were unlocked, twenty more people had joined the queue. Once inside, Kate waited less than three minutes to reach the window. She wrote out a check for twenty thousand dollars. "I'd like to cash this." She presented her ID to the teller.

"I'm sorry, but the limit on cash withdrawals is $2,000." The teller inspected the check. "I can issue a bank check for the remainder."

Kate knew better than to ask *why*. "No thanks. I'll write another check. Is the limit per day or per transaction, when is the next time I can make a withdrawal?"

"Per customer, per day." The teller watched Kate write out a new check.

Kate waited for the teller to count her money, then quickly hit the ATM for another $500 on the way to her car. She said aloud to herself, "The system didn't block me from cashing a check and hitting the ATM. I wonder if I could cash another check at a different branch."

Kate hurried to the next branch north on Peachtree Road. By the time she arrived, the line was out the door and into the parking lot. "Rats! They'll be out of money by the time I get to the window." She felt anxious, wishing she'd been more proactive. "I should have followed my instincts. I should have taken out more money when I could."

She sat in the parking lot for a moment. Her mind raced to think of other alternatives. She remembered Bill's advice about silver and gold. "I suppose I could go buy some coins with my debit card. I'm sure I'll take a bath on the resale if nothing happens. But if everything falls apart and I don't, I'll be kicking myself again."

Kate checked her phone for the nearest gold coin dealer. "Wow. This place is on the way back to my house." She hastily turned around and headed south on Peachtree. Minutes later, she pulled into the parking lot of the coin dealer. Kate took a deep breath to calm herself before going in.

She opened the door and was greeted by a guy who looked too young to be running a coin shop.

"How can I help you?"

"Do you take debit cards?" She tried not to sound frantic.

"We do. But our margins are low, so we have to pass on the credit card fees to the buyer. We add an extra 3.5% for plastic."

She looked at the coins in the case. "I understand."

"Are you looking for anything in particular?"

"I'm looking for something that will hold its value—but as close to the raw material price as possible, not necessarily a collectible."

"Bullion, then. Gold or silver?"

"I don't know. I'm looking to spend like 20 thousand."

"Oh, okay." The young man's eyes lit up. "Twenty thousand dollars in gold bullion will fit in a plastic tube that you can carry with one hand. Twenty thousand in silver is going to weigh roughly 70 pounds. So, logistics is going to be a factor in your decision."

"Hmm." Kate considered the implications. "Let's go with gold."

"Okay, bars are the cheapest alternative for straight bullion. While they are slightly more expensive, Canadian Maple Leaves and American Eagles are still considered bullion."

"Can I take a look?"

"Sure." The salesman took out a tray. "This is a privately minted one-ounce gold bar."

Kate inspected the object.

"And these are the coins minted by their respective nations."

Kate held each of the coins in plastic sleeves. "Can I split it up evenly?"

"Sure. You could do five of each. That would take you just over 20 thousand, total."

"How much over?"

He entered some numbers on his calculator. "Roughly seven hundred dollars."

She pulled out her bank card. "Okay."

"And I will need an ID for a purchase this large."

"Sure." She placed her driver's license on the counter.

The man totaled her purchases and ran the card. "I'm sorry, it's not accepting your card."

She rummaged through her wallet and retrieved two credit cards. "Can you put half on each of these?"

"I'll try." The man swiped the cards and watched the machine spit out the vouchers for Kate's signature. He gently placed the gold into a small cardboard box with the store's name and logo on the top. "Thank you so much."

"You, too. Have a good day." Kate hurried out the door and tried to call Sky National Bank to see what was wrong with her debit card while she walked to the car. She received an *all-lines-are-busy* message and hung up.

She started the engine and headed toward her

apartment. She dialed Terry's number, but the call went straight to voicemail. She didn't leave a message.

She soon arrived home and took the elevator up to her floor. Kate's phone rang. It was Terry. "Hey, I just tried to call you."

"Yeah, I saw. I guess you heard what happened at work."

"No. I haven't heard anything."

"The viruses activated. All the bank's data has been encrypted."

"So, it's a ransomware attack?"

"As far as I know, no one is asking for ransom."

Her phone beeped. "I'm getting a call on the other line. It's Mendoza. Can I call you back?"

"Yeah. But call me right back."

She switched over. "Mr. Mendoza, hi."

"Kate. We need you to come in. How long will it take you to get here?"

"Depending on traffic, an hour maybe. I'm not dressed for work."

"Don't worry about what you look like. This is an emergency. Have you heard what's going on?"

She wasn't sure if Terry was supposed to tell her what he knew. "No, sir. What's happening?"

"The malicious code has been activated. It's encrypted all of our data. All customer accounts, bank records, employee files, the website, everything."

"Is the NSA still there?"

"Yeah, they're the ones who called me. They're allowing me to bring in our best and brightest to try and decrypt the files."

Kate quickly pulled out a nice top that would go with the jeans she was already wearing. She changed while talking to Mendoza on the phone. "They had full control of our network all weekend. They couldn't stop the attack?"

Mendoza sounded perturbed. "I'm not so sure they didn't do something to inadvertently trigger the virus. But I suppose we shouldn't be talking about it, especially over the phone. I'll see you when you get here.

"And remember, Albert has them all worked up over his little stunt last night, so don't speak to them unless spoken to. If they ask you anything, keep your answers short."

"But we're helping them, right?"

"Yes, but they may not be as appreciative as they should be."

Kate frowned. "I'll be in as soon as possible, Mr. Mendoza."

CHAPTER 12

And it shall come to pass, that in all the land, saith the Lord, two parts therein shall be cut off and die; but the third shall be left therein. And I will bring the third part through the fire, and will refine them as silver is refined, and will try them as gold is tried: they shall call on my name, and I will hear them: I will say, it is my people: and they shall say, the Lord is my God.

Zechariah 13:8-9

Kate swiped her badge across the access sensor for the Information Security Control Center. Out of habit she placed her hand on the door handle and pulled. The sensor flashed red. "Denied, great!" She pounded on the heavy metal door with the back of her fist.

The door opened. "Come in." She recognized the NSA agent as being the tech who'd debriefed her.

"Oscar, right?"

"Yes. Thanks for coming in."

Kate looked around. She recognized only Quinton, Linda, and Rodney from her team. The other ten or so workers appeared to be NSA employees. "Albert is really good with this kind of thing. Is he coming in?"

Oscar looked at her like a child who was asking for ice cream before dinner. "For all we know, the attackers upped their launch time because Albert decided to cash in his fifteen minutes of fame last night. He's in hot water."

It was the answer she expected. "So, what can I do?"

"Are you any good at cracking encryption?"

"If I have the key."

Oscar sighed. "Yeah, that makes two of us." He led her to a terminal. "Take a look and let me know what you think."

She looked at the random string of numbers, letters, and symbols. "Looks like 256 bit."

"Yeah. Any other insight you can provide?"

While she watched, the characters all changed. "Wait! Did you see that?"

"Yeah, they all just flipped. What was that?"

"I think the data just got another layer of encryption. When did the first layer of encryption happen?"

Oscar looked at his watch. "One hour ago."

Kate thought about where she was one hour earlier. The data must have been encrypted seconds before the salesman at the coin shop swiped her debit card. "I hope the data isn't re-encrypting every hour. You'll never get this thing figured out. You haven't received any demands from the attackers?"

"Not yet."

Oscar's phone vibrated. He answered, "Hello?"

He was silent for a moment. "Bank of America and Chase?"

Kate guessed what was happening. "Call the FDIC and the Chairman of the Fed. They need to convince all the remaining banks to power off their servers. You'll have a better chance of recovering their data if you unplug the networks before everything is encrypted."

Oscar nodded at her then said to the person on the other line, "Did you get that?"

He was quiet for a second. "Yes, I concur with her assessment. Call me when it's done."

Oscar hung up and rubbed his head.

"We should shut down our network. At least it can't add another layer of encryption every hour if it's unplugged." Kate looked at the computer monitor.

"Okay. Do it."

Kate stood up from the desk. "I can't even enter a command on this thing. The mainframes are in the basement. We'll have to physically throw the breakers."

Oscar followed her out the door and to the elevator. "Where are your backups stored?"

"Jungle Cloud Services. The same place as most

every other bank. I can't imagine the hackers would have gone through so much trouble to hit at least three major banks and not penetrate the cloud servers. Maybe you can convince them to power down."

"Jungle? Are you serious? That would take down about thirty percent of the internet." The elevator doors opened and Oscar followed Kate down a narrow hall lit by buzzing fluorescent lights.

"All the banks should be on dedicated servers. They should be able to selectively power down only those." She held her badge over the access sensor. It flashed red.

Oscar held up his badge. "Allow me." The light turned green and the lock clicked open.

Kate sprinted between a canyon of server racks buzzing and blinking with life. Finally, she reached the breaker box. She threw the main power lever and the rows of black metal boxes behind her fell dark and quiet. "It's done."

"Now what?"

"Let's get those backup files and see if they're infected." Kate marched back toward the elevator.

"What hardware are you planning to use?" Oscar asked.

"I have equipment at home."

"No way, NSA will never allow you to take this home."

"Then I guess I'm done. Everything here is fried." Kate pressed the elevator's call button.

"We'll bring in our own hardware." Oscar followed her into the lift.

"Call me when you get it set up." She stepped

out into the lobby.

Before the door closed to take Oscar up to the ISCC he said, "Don't forget, everything you know about the situation falls under the National Security Letter."

She didn't turn around. America's banking system was collapsing and the only thing the NSA seemed to care about was controlling the narrative. She wondered if Albert had been right to blow the whistle. Either way, she was done. They'd created this mess, let them clean it up.

Kate called Terry. "Hey, you should try to get out of work early."

"Why? What happened?"

She knew better than to elaborate on the phone. "I was just reminded that I'm not allowed to talk about it. But take my advice. I can't imagine you have anything worthwhile to do anyway."

Terry said, "I've got the financial services team calling all of our high-end clientele to reassure them that we have the situation under control and that their accounts should be restored soon."

"So, you're overseeing a cover-up operation."

"Nothing good is going to come of letting people panic."

She replied, "Nothing good will come of lying to them either."

"Okay, let me wrap this up. What are you going to do?"

"I'll meet you at your house." Kate clicked off the phone and rushed to her car.

Once home, she feverishly shoved some clothes

and her hygiene essentials into her suitcase. She zipped it up and placed it by the door. Next, she jabbed her cash, new coin collection, and shotgun shells into her backpack and headed out the door.

Kate was back in her car in a matter of minutes. She turned on the radio and scrolled through the stations. She finally came across a news report.

"Wells Fargo and Citi Bank have officially been added to the list of corporations which were hacked in today's massive attack against the banking system. The total count is currently at twenty-seven institutions and includes all the largest financial companies in America.

"Pundits who discounted the caveat issued on last night's edition of 60 Minutes have been proven wrong in spades. In addition to the banks, credit card processing centers have suspended services until they can determine if their systems have been infected by the viruses. The breach is being labeled as Locust Swarm because of the explanation given by the Sky National Bank whistleblower, Albert Rogers.

"The US Treasury issued a statement moments ago assuring the public that, despite Albert Rodgers' warning of Cyber Armageddon, this incident will prove to have been nothing more than a temporary glitch. The Treasury Secretary and the FDIC Chairman will be holding a joint press conference at the White House briefing room this afternoon at 2:30.

"Some bank customers seem hesitant to buy into the reassurances. Police have been called to multiple branch locations around the country to break up irate bank depositors who are demanding their money."

Kate glanced down at her fuel gauge. "I should have filled up on the way back from Waynesville. I better get gas now." She pulled into the next filling station. All the pumps had hand-written cardboard signs taped to them which read, *Cash only. Pay inside.*

She stepped out of her vehicle and walked in. Two customers were yelling at the attendant, insisting that he accept their credit cards.

"Please leave before I call the police!" The attendant seemed to have run out of patience.

"There you go! Call the cops!" yelled one of the customers. "How about I give you something to call them over!" He swept his hand across the shelf, knocking boxes of candy bars and gum onto the floor on his way out the door.

The other man stood with his arms crossed, grimacing angrily.

"Excuse me." Kate stepped past him and pulled out two 20-dollar bills from her backpack. "Can you put this on pump three, please?"

"Sure." The attendant took her cash and rang up the sale.

Kate hurried to exit the heated atmosphere in the gas station. She checked her phone while the pump dispensed the fuel into her tank.

Suddenly, she felt an abrupt jerk from behind. Someone had pulled her backpack from off her shoulder. "Stop!" she screamed. She abandoned the pump and sprinted toward the man who was running away with her pack over his shoulder. Kate recognized him as the man from inside the store who'd watched her pay with cash. She was sure he had no idea of the prize he'd just claimed. Her pack contained several thousand dollars in cash along with $20 thousand in gold coins and bars.

Kate closed the distance, but the man was still far from her. She could not, would not give up! Her legs pumped hard against the pavement. Six months of Jiu-Jitsu had not only increased her confidence, but the routine warm ups had also greatly increased her cardiovascular capacity. She saw the man tiring within the first minutes of the chase.

Then, he ran into the intersection and had to stop short to avoid being hit by a car. Kate saw her chance. She grabbed the strap of the backpack and latched on tight. Next, she put her arm around his waist, tucked low, and spun him around, pulling him to the ground. Kate landed on top of the man's chest. He reached up and grabbed her throat with both hands, constricting his fingers around her windpipe.

Kate quickly grabbed his right hand, spun her left leg over his face, squeezed her knees together to pinch his bicep, held his wrist with his thumb facing the sky and laid back.

SNAP! His elbow popped, allowing his forearm to extend much farther back than normal. "Ahhhww!" He screeched in agony.

Kate wasted no time. He was down, but not out. She crossed her arms, grabbed the side of his collar with one hand, then the rear of his collar with the other and pulled, forcing his throat ever tighter against her wrist and forearm. Seconds later, he ceased his struggle to get free from her grasp. Kate collected her belongings and left the attacker asleep in the road.

When she returned to her car, the pump had clicked off at $40. She quickly returned the pump and tightened her gas cap. She intended to be long gone by the time her attacker woke up.

CHAPTER 13

Behold, the day of the Lord cometh, and thy spoil shall be divided in the midst of thee.

Zechariah 14:1

Kate rang the doorbell and pounded on Terry's door. Penny answered. "Kate! What's wrong? Are you okay?"

Kate broke down in tears. "No. I'm not okay. Some guy at the gas station snatched my bag off my shoulder and ran off with it."

Penny pulled her close. "You poor thing." She pushed her back. "Let's have a look at you. Did you call the police?"

"No, I just wanted to get out of there before he woke up."

"What do you mean?"

"I chased him down, put him in an armbar and snapped his elbow. Then I put him in a cross-collar choke and he went out."

Penny covered her mouth with eyes wide open. "Kate! You could have been killed! Why didn't you just let him have your bag?"

"It had all my money in it. I should have split it up, but I didn't think. I was in a hurry to get over here. Are the kids home from school yet?"

Penny shook her head. "No, why would they be?"

"It's chaos out there, Penny. You need to go get Sam and Vicky from school before it gets worse."

"Just calm down. Let me get you a drink of water." Penny walked to the kitchen. "You've been through a very traumatic event."

"Penny, what happened to me is nothing. Things are about to get a lot worse. Terry is on his way home now. We're going straight to the cabin in Waynesville. You need to get bags packed for the kids so we can get out before dark."

Penny opened the plastic bottle of water for Kate. "Would you like a glass?"

"No, Penny, I don't want a glass. I want you to take this seriously."

Penny placed the bottle of water on the counter and took a seat on a nearby stool. "Listen, Kate. You had a bad experience. I'll give you that. And I'm very sorry it happened to you. But it just goes to show what happens when people lose their heads over these types of situations. The government has everything under control. This thing will be sorted out in a day or two. The best thing we can do is stay here and relax. The more people who are out on the roads feeling afraid and letting their emotions get the better of them, the worse off we'll all be."

"Penny, the government isn't going to sort anything out."

"Didn't that guy who was on 60 Minutes last night work with you?"

"Yes, and the government is going to lock him up for what he said. He told you what I can't say. Look, everything he said would happen is coming true. Can't you see?"

Penny crossed her arms and gave Kate a condescending look. "What I see is that he incited panic in a handful of weak-minded individuals. One of whom attacked you because he thought the sky was falling in. This Albert guy *should* be locked up. Freedom of speech doesn't allow you to yell fire in a theater."

"You can if there really is a fire." Kate chugged her drink and tossed the bottle in the trash. "Thanks for the water. I'll wait for Terry outside."

"Kate!" Penny followed her to the door. "Don't be like that. You're upset. Come sit down and try to relax."

"I'll wait for my brother outside." Kate pulled the door closed behind her.

Once outside, she leaned against the hood of her car and called Terry.

"Hey, what's up?"

"I'm at your house. Penny acts like she doesn't know what's going on at all. Have you talked to her?"

"You're already there? And yes, I did speak with

her. At least I tried. She thinks it will all blow over."

"But you know it won't. You have to convince her to start packing, Terry. She hasn't pulled the kids out of school, she hasn't even packed a bag for her or anyone else. We have to get out of here soon. We need to be at the cabin before dark. She isn't taking this seriously at all."

Terry sighed. "We'll talk when I get there. But take it easy with Penny. You know how she is, the harder you push her, the harder she pushes back. You have to convince her that it's her idea if you want her to do something."

"We don't have time for all of that, Terry! She needs to step aside and let you lead for once."

"Leave her alone until I get home. I'm on the road now."

"You should gas up before you come home. People are already getting edgy. My bag got snatched at the pump so stay alert of your surroundings."

"Your bag got snatched?"

"Yeah, I got it back and I'm fine. Long story. I'll tell you when you get here." She clicked off the phone and waited. For the next fifteen minutes, Kate clicked through various news websites, which were already beginning to report on localized outbreaks of violence and looting across the country.

"Aunt Kate, hey! What are you doing here?" Victoria came walking up the driveway with her older brother close behind her.

"Hey, Vicky. Hi, Sam. I'm just waiting for your

dad."

Penny stuck her head out the door. "Kids, come on in the house."

"I'm just saying hi to my aunt," Vicky protested.

"Please, Victoria. Don't argue with me. I need your help with something."

"Go ahead. It's alright." Kate smiled, but inside she knew Penny didn't want her poisoning the minds of her children by exposing them to reality.

"Are you staying for dinner?" Sam walked by.

"I'm not sure. We'll see." Kate waved at the siblings.

Half an hour later, Terry pulled into the drive.

Kate approached his car. "Did you get gas?"

"No. Two stations were out of gas; two others were closed and the police were at another. Penny's Escalade is three-quarters full. *If* we leave, we'll take the SUV."

"*If* we leave? What are you talking about *if*? We have to go, Terry. And we have to go now!"

He held up a hand. "I know. But give me a little time. I need to get her to come around. Like I said, no one is going to force her to do anything she doesn't want to do."

"But your kids, this place is going to melt down into a war zone!"

Terry grunted. "Come on in. We'll get something to eat, and I'll try to convince her. Tell me about what happened at the gas station."

Reluctantly, Kate followed her brother into the house and described her encounter.

Excited, Vicky met her at the door. "Are you eating dinner with us?"

"Yes, I guess so."

Penny dropped some pasta into a pot of boiling water on the stove. "We're so happy to have you join us, Kate, but let's try to avoid any distressing topics while we eat. We don't want to ruin the meal."

Kate looked at her brother as if to implore him to say something. But, he did not.

He hugged his kids, then kissed Penny. "After dinner, we'll watch the news. We'll assess the situation and make a decision about what to do then."

"Please, Terry, not in front of the children." Penny diced some garlic, threw it into a sauté pan, and drizzled olive oil on top of it.

Sam's mouth hung open. "Mom! I can drive. In two years, I can be drafted and sent to a foreign country to kill people for a living. I'm not a kid."

"And even if I'm younger, I'm more mature." Vicky laughed.

"Sam, don't say things like that. Nobody is sending you to a foreign country to kill anybody." Penny shook her head and tossed some fresh spinach in with the garlic and oil. She wiped her hands on a dish towel and turned to Terry. "Besides, there's nothing to discuss anyway. This whole thing is going to blow over." She gestured toward the television. "The Treasury Secretary, the Fed Chairman, and the head of the FDIC were all on the press conference just a little while ago. They said everything will be back to normal in no time at all."

"They're in crisis management mode. They'll say anything to keep the peace," Kate said.

Penny pursed her lips. "They also said fear itself is the only real danger. If people allow themselves to panic, things could get a little precarious. But as long as we stay around the house until things quiet down, we'll be fine."

"You don't know that." Kate crossed her arms.

Penny stirred the pan. "And I suppose you know more than the Treasury, the Federal Reserve, and the FDIC."

"I can't talk about what I know. But what I can tell you is that they are lying through their teeth." Kate scowled.

Vicky took a seat on the bar stool at the counter. "What do you mean you can't talk about it? Did you get one of those thingies, like the guy on the news last night? What's it called, Sam?"

He looked at his phone and shrugged. "I can't remember, a National Security Memo or something?"

"National Security Letter," Terry corrected. "And anyone who gets one can't even say they got one, so please don't ask your aunt about it."

Vicky clapped her hands together loudly. "You did get one! You worked with that guy. Was he telling the truth?"

Penny turned from the stove, wooden spatula in hand. "He was not telling the truth. He was trying to frighten people, and we're not the sort who fall for those types of shenanigans. Now drop the subject this instant! I don't want to hear another word about it!" She pointed the spatula at everyone in the room. "From any of you!"

"This is totally unrelated." Sam looked at his

phone. "But there's a flash mob running through Lenox Square right now. They're stealing anything and everything."

"It's on Facebook?" Vicky looked at his phone.

"Yep. Live stream."

"See where all this kind of talk leads?" Penny shook the spatula at Terry.

"Penny, reasonable people talking about taking precautions against a very real threat doesn't cause riots," Kate tried to persuade.

"Let's try to show a little faith." Penny resumed stirring the pan.

"Faith in what?" Kate was confused.

"God," Penny replied matter-of-factly.

Kate countered, "God? You go to church on Christmas and Easter."

"When do you go, Kate?" Penny's reply was sharp.

"Christmas and Easter."

"Then why would you act like it's a problem if those are also the times I choose to go?"

Kate lifted her shoulders. "I'm just saying, you don't exactly lead a pious life, not that I do either. But it seems strange to be talking about faith right now."

"Why is that strange, Kate?"

"I've never heard about burglaries in this neighborhood, yet you lock your doors at night. You have fire insurance. I'm sure Terry handles that, but I've never heard you give him a hard time about it. You have health insurance also, I assume. For all of these far-lesser threats, you take measures to hedge your risk. But suddenly when the world starts coming unglued, you're putting the fate of your family in the hands of someone you visit twice a year."

"Kate, I asked you to drop the subject. You're a guest in my home. I would appreciate it if you would respect my wishes."

"Okay." Kate walked out of the room.

Terry followed her to the living room where he turned on the cable news channel. "See what I'm dealing with?"

"Yeah, but what are you going to do about it? Are you going to risk the lives of your kids because your wife wants to stick her head in the sand?"

"Whatever we do, we have to stay together."

"Yes. We have to stick together, and we have to leave. We should have already left. No credit cards, no banks, how long do you think it will be before the grocery stores run out of food? Credit is the lifeblood of the American economy. Everything is about to come to a grinding halt."

"I've got probably a month's worth of food in the house."

"What if it doesn't blow over in a month? And besides, hardly anyone else has food stored. This mob is raiding the mall six hours after the viruses struck. They're not hungry or desperate. They're just causing trouble because they can get away with it. What do you think they'll do when their fridge is empty? I'll tell you what they'll do. They'll do exactly what they are doing now, but they'll go from house to house doing whatever they want looking for food."

Terry rubbed his chin. "What am I going to do?

Leave my wife?"

"If you have to, in order to save your children, then yes. But that's her choice. Not yours. If everyone else is packing up, I doubt she'll want to stay here by herself."

He shook his head. "You have no idea how she'd be if I make an ultimatum like that."

"You don't have a choice, Terry. You can't sacrifice your kids because you want to please your wife."

He gave a sigh of defeat. "Let's hope she'll come around to our way of thinking after she hears the local news. I'm sure it won't be good."

She pleaded with him. "Yeah, then everyone else and their grandma will be on the road trying to get out of town. It will be gridlock. You know what Atlanta traffic is like on a normal workday. What do you think it will be like with half of the city trying to get out of Dodge at the same time?"

Terry ran his hands from the top of his head down his face. "I know, Kate. But I can't just leave my wife."

CHAPTER 14

I beheld the earth, and, lo, it was without form, and void; and the heavens, and they had no light. I beheld the mountains, and, lo, they trembled, and all the hills moved lightly. I beheld, and, lo, there was no man, and all the birds of the heavens were fled. I beheld, and, lo, the fruitful place was a wilderness, and all the cities thereof were broken down at the presence of the Lord, and by his fierce anger. For thus hath the Lord said, The whole land shall be desolate; yet will I not make a full end. For this shall the earth mourn, and the heavens above be black; because I have spoken it, I have purposed it, and will not repent, neither will I turn back from it.

Jeremiah 4:23-28

Dinner was tense. Conversations were stilted and artificial, serving only to dissipate the awkward silence. Kate spoke only when spoken to.

"The pasta was great, honey. If you'll excuse me, I'm going to catch the local news." Terry stood up from the table.

"I'll join you." Penny placed her napkin on her plate. "Vicky, will you and your brother get the dishes this evening?"

"I want to know what's going on also," Vicky protested.

Penny pushed in her chair. "I'm sure they'll be talking about it all evening. The news channels will milk this one as long as they can."

Sam began collecting the plates from the table. "Let's just hurry up and get it finished."

"Thank you for dinner, Penny. And thanks for cleaning up, guys." Kate smiled at her niece and nephew.

"No problem, Aunt Kate. But if we go to the cabin I'm riding with you," Vicky stated.

"Fair enough." Kate followed her brother and sister-in-law to the den where the news had already begun.

"The mayor of Atlanta has issued a city-wide curfew to go into effect at sunset this evening and will remain in place until sunrise tomorrow morning. A spokesperson for the mayor's office said that the move is a preemptive attempt to quell social unrest which is brewing around the city.

"Our station has received multiple reports of looting and confrontations between businesses and patrons over the ongoing credit card and banking crisis.

"Federal authorities have gone out of their way to put the public at ease by assuring us that the situation will be rectified shortly. Nevertheless, it only takes a handful of people who are unable to access basic goods and services to spread a sense of general unease throughout the population.

"As the contagion worsens, we are hearing of more and more shop owners deciding to close their doors to avoid additional conflict with enraged customers unable to purchase necessary items like food and gas. With each new closure, even those who are able to pay with cash cannot buy the fundamental supplies they need for the day.

"This is all so ridiculous." Penny sat on the sofa next to Terry and rolled her eyes.

Kate looked at the time on her phone. "We have about two hours before the curfew begins. This is our last chance to leave tonight."

Terry said, "It looks like things are getting bad. Penny, why don't you go ahead and put a few things in a bag. We'll go to the cabin tonight. If things blow over, we can come right back tomorrow. I'll tell the kids."

Penny crossed her arms and let her mouth hang open. "Are you serious? The news basically said the only reason the streets are dangerous is because people are giving into panic. I don't want to feed into this hysteria. Besides, we're in the safest place we could possibly be."

Terry gave a contrived grin. "Kate, can you give us a few minutes to talk?"

"Sure, I'll help the kids finish up the dishes." Kate ascended the stairs and made her way back to the kitchen. "Can I help?"

"We're finished," Sam pressed the start button on the dishwasher.

"What's going on with Mom and Dad? Are we leaving?" Vicky leaned against the counter.

"They're having a discussion about that right now." Kate leaned next to her.

"What if Mom and Dad don't go? Are you still going to the cabin tonight?" Sam asked.

Kate thought about the question. She knew she probably should, but this was her family. "No. Whatever we do, we need to do it together."

Vicky hugged her. "Thanks, Aunt Kate."

Minutes later, Kate walked to the top of the stairs to see if Terry and Penny had reached a resolution. She overheard Penny speaking.

"I love Kate like my own sister, but I don't want to uproot my family because of her delusional paranoia. I understand she has mental issues, but I can't allow that to be a problem in my house. And you are making it worse by playing along with all of this craziness."

She could hear Terry's reply. "It's not craziness, Penny. I've never seen a curfew issued in Atlanta, this is a legitimate emergency. Why are you fighting me on this? And Kate has social anxiety disorder, she's not schizophrenic. Quit making her out to be a lunatic."

Kate wanted no part of that conversation. She returned to the kitchen where Vicky and Sam were monitoring the events around Atlanta via social media.

"No way! Check this out!" Sam held up his phone for Kate to see video of a massive fire burning.

"Where is that?" Kate looked closer.

"The Mercedes Benz dealership." Sam turned the phone back toward himself.

"The one in Buckhead?" Kate was concerned that it could be so close.

"Yep." Sam continued to watch his screen.

Vicky ran to the back door and opened it. "I bet we can smell the smoke from here!"

"Let's keep the door closed." Kate pulled the door shut.

"Why? What do you think can happen?" Vicky looked curiously at her aunt.

"Probably nothing. But just in case the ne'er-do-wells venture out this way, we don't want to give them the opportunity to pull anything."

"You think looters are going to come to our neighborhood?" Sam seemed skeptical.

Kate said, "I hope not. But if you were going to loot houses, where would you go?"

"Buckhead," Vicky replied matter-of-factly.

"You're right," said Sam.

Terry stormed up the stairs, his face in a bad-tempered pucker. "Kate, we're going to wait until morning to see how things are going. The news just showed the traffic on I-85 and I-75. They both look like parking lots."

"We'd take US-19. We wouldn't have to get on the interstate."

"I know, but 19 could be locked up as well from people trying to avoid the interstates. Anyway, you can take the guest room downstairs. I'm going to get a shower and try to relax in my room." He tried to smile. "Good night. We'll figure it out tomorrow."

Vicky looked concerned about her dad's mood. "Good night, Daddy. I hope you sleep well."

"You, too, sweetheart."

"I love you, Dad." Sam waved.

"You, too, buddy." Terry disappeared down the hall.

"He looks mad." Vicky's brows sank low.

"He'll be okay." Kate pulled her close for a hug. "Your dad gets upset, but he gets over it fast."

"Was he like that when you guys were growing up?" Sam asked.

"Yeah."

"Because of Uncle Boyd?" Vicky inquired?

"Usually." Kate laughed. "I'm going to get some stuff out of my car."

"Can we watch TV with you?" Vicky asked.

"Sure. Give me a half hour to brush my teeth and get a shower, then you two come on down." Kate walked out the back door. She could hear the roar of police and fire sirens in the distance. "It's going to be a long night." She popped the trunk of her Mini and retrieved her pack and the soft rifle case which held her father's old shotgun.

Kate stayed up late watching the local news with her niece and nephew. The Atlanta station aired a special broadcast to cover the deteriorating conditions around the city, suspending regular programming and continuing their coverage from the 5:00 o'clock edition through to the 10:00 PM broadcast.

The news told of widespread looting, including smash and grabs at a variety of retail establishments such as liquor stores and convenience stores that had closed down due to the ongoing credit card outages. Criminal activity became too out of hand for police to control and the chaos began to creep into residential streets.

A loud knock came to the door.

"Who could that be?" Vicky sat at the foot of Kate's bed in the guest room looking at her brother who was watching the news from the small easy chair.

"Beats me. Are you going to go look?"

"I'll go." Kate pulled the shotgun out from beneath the bed.

"You have a gun?" Vicky looked astonished.

"It was your grandfather's." Kate began climbing the stairs with Vicky and Sam right behind her.

Terry was already at the door, looking out the peephole.

"Who is it?" Vicky asked.

"It's your friend from school, Amanda." Terry stepped back and unlocked the door.

A frantic and crying girl ran in the house. "Mr. McCarthy, you have to help! They came in my house! They attacked my dad! He told me to run out the back door and come here!"

Vicky grabbed her friend and hugged her. "It's okay, you're safe."

"You have to help my dad!" Amanda sobbed.

Penny walked into the room with her housecoat on. "What's going on? What's happening?"

"Let me just grab my shoes and a jacket. I'll come with you to help your dad." Terry darted off to his bedroom.

"Terry! There's a curfew. You can't go out. Just call the police! They'll handle this." Penny trailed off behind him.

Terry was back in a matter of moments. "Come on, Amanda. I'll drive."

"I'm coming with you." Vicky stepped into her tennis shoes.

Terry shook his head. "No. You are staying here. Lock the doors and stay inside until we get back."

"I'm coming," Kate declared.

Terry glanced at the pump-action shotgun. "Okay. Kate, ride in the back. Amanda, you ride up front with me so you can show me where you live."

"Terry! You are not leaving this house!" Penny insisted.

Terry ran towards the Escalade without addressing his wife. Amanda got in the front, and Kate took the back. Once out of the drive, Terry asked, "Where do you live?"

"Christian Park, on Blanton," Amanda said between sobs.

"Is that close by?" Kate asked.

"Three streets over. I can't believe everything

broke down this fast." Terry drove feverishly.

"People saw Albert's interview. They know the government is lying about the virus being patched. They're starting to put two and two together. No money, no credit cards means no food, no booze, no cigarettes. Pretty soon the trucks will stop rolling, police are already overwhelmed. They'll have to make choices about whether to go home and try to protect their own families or risk it all to fight a losing battle. People who are already living on the edge are doing what they have to do to make sure they get theirs."

Terry turned to Amanda. "How many people came into your house?"

"I'm not sure. Three I think. One had a crowbar that he used to pull the door open. Another had a ball bat. I saw my dad get hit." The girl continued to cry as they drove down her street. "That's my house, the white one on the left."

Terry pulled in. Kate could see from the back seat that the front door was still open. She jumped out and followed Terry up to the front porch.

"I've got a gun! If there's anyone in here that shouldn't be, this is your last chance to get out alive!" Kate couldn't believe those words were coming out of her mouth. But she knew it was true. She was a bit skittish under normal conditions, so if she felt threatened while she had a shotgun in her hand, she'd certainly shoot first and ask questions later.

Amanda ran past Terry and Kate. "Dad!"

Kate followed her to the dining room where her father lay on the floor bleeding from the back of his head.

Terry rushed in and bent down by the man. He checked his pulse and looked up at Amanda. "He's alive. Kate, call 911."

Kate held the shotgun with one hand and dialed the number. "All circuits are busy."

"We have to get him to the hospital." Terry tossed his keys to Kate. "Pull the Escalade up in the front yard. Back up as close to the front door as possible."

Kate looked around to make sure she didn't hear or see any looters still in the house before leaving her unarmed brother in the house. "Okay. Piedmont is closest."

"No way. The closer we get to downtown, the worse it will be. We'll take him to Northside."

Kate ran to get the SUV.

Amanda helped Terry to get her father into the back of the Escalade.

"Stay with him," Terry ordered Amanda, then ran to the passenger's seat. "I'll take the shotgun. You drive. Treat red lights like stop signs and don't stop for anything else." Terry slammed the door shut.

Kate put the SUV in gear. She sped north on Lake Forest Drive, encountering only a handful of police cars with their lights and sirens heading in the opposite direction. Each time she saw another set of lights in the distance racing toward her, she tensed up, thinking about the worst possible scenario where she and Terry were arrested for being out past curfew. She knew it was ridiculous and that any reasonable police officer would know she was only trying to help, but she couldn't help thinking what if?

Once at the hospital, Terry ran in the emergency room entrance. He came out minutes later with two nurses and a gurney. Amanda got out of the vehicle and followed the workers into the hospital. Terry got back in the passenger's seat. "You okay to drive?"

Kate watched Amanda's father being wheeled away. "Yeah, are we just going to leave them?"

"We've done all we can for them. I need to get home, load my family up and get out of here." Terry examined the bloodstains on his shirt.

"I can drive." Kate put the Escalade in gear and punched the accelerator. Emergency vehicles speeding south passed her on the road back. She could see the glow of large fires against low-hanging clouds from multiple locations in the distance. She smelled the smoke and soot. They quickly returned to Terry's house.

"Back up in the front yard, right to the door. I want to get loaded up as quickly as possible." Terry bailed out of the vehicle and slammed the door.

Kate cut the ignition, exited the vehicle and followed close behind her brother.

Penny opened the front door. She focused on the bloodstains which soiled Terry's shirt. "What happened to you?"

"It's not my blood."

"Where is Amanda?" Vicky waited inside the doorway.

"She's fine. She stayed with her father at the hospital." Kate hugged her.

"Her dad, is he going to make it?" Vicky begged.

"He was unconscious, but he was breathing good and had a strong heartbeat. He should be okay. We took him to Northside. They'll take good care of him." Terry pulled his daughter close and kissed the top of her head. "But for now, I need everyone to pack a bag. We're going to the cabin. I want to be out of here in twenty minutes." Terry clapped his hands at his children. "Come on, let's go! Right now!"

Vicky and Sam stared at him with eyes wide, then hustled off to their respective rooms.

Penny crossed her arms. "Terry! It's the middle of the night! We can't go now. There's a curfew!"

"And the police are obviously unable to enforce it. We're leaving, and we're leaving right now. Pack a bag, Penny." His face was hard.

"I'm not going anywhere." She pulled the collar of her housecoat up around her neck and began to walk away.

"Then stay here, but I'm taking the kids. And I'm taking the Escalade. I'll leave the Mercedes for you."

"You're not taking the kids!"

"This is not a discussion. I'm taking the kids if I have to duct tape you to a chair. I should have listened to my sister and left before the news came on. But I didn't. Now we're all in danger."

"And I suppose that's my fault." Penny stood defiantly with her hands on her hips.

"No. It's my fault. I never should have capitulated to your demands. And now I'm through talking about it. I'm going to get a quick shower to wash the blood off of me, then I'm leaving with the kids. Do whatever you want, but I'm warning you, don't get in my way with the kids."

Kate avoided looking at either one of them.

"I hope you're happy now, Kate. You got your way." Penny stormed off to the bedroom.

Kate grimaced.

"Don't worry about her. It's certainly not your fault." Terry gave her a quick squeeze.

Kate forced a smile. "Thanks. I've got walkie-talkies in the car so we can stay in contact on the road."

Terry said, "Good. I'll drive up front. You trail behind me. If you don't mind, I'd appreciate it if you'd let the kids ride with you. If we come across a threat, I can handle that. You just worry about getting my kids out of there."

"Sure, no problem. I'll get the radios set up. Do you want those extra dry goods loaded into the Escalade?"

"Yeah, that would be great." Terry hurried off to get his shower and pack.

Twenty minutes later, Kate pulled a box of shotgun shells out of her pack. She put five shells in her left front pocket and placed the rest in the center console of her Mini. She pulled her hair back into a ponytail and fished it through the opening of her ball cap. She positioned the pump-action shotgun between the console and the passenger's seat.

Kate opened the trunk of her vehicle. "Vicky, you and your brother are riding with me. You can put your bags in here."

Vicky looked stressed. She tossed her belongings into the back of Kate's car.

CHAPTER 15

The spoilers are come upon all high places through the wilderness: for the sword of the Lord shall devour from the one end of the land even to the other end of the land: no flesh shall have peace.

Jeremiah 12:12

Kate raised the shotgun putting the front bead on the torso of the man who was about to kill Terry. Her hands shook with terror, her stomach constricted.
BOOOOM!
The impact of the shot slammed the man to the ground.
"That came from the trees!" The driver pointed

in Kate's direction and drew his pistol. "Start shooting right there!"

Kate quickly moved out of the way before the remaining three men began taking pot shots in her direction.

POW! Bang! Crack!

She pumped another shell into the chamber. Sprinting in the dark, her foot caught a fallen branch and she fell face first onto the forest floor. "Umph!"

"Right there! I saw someone moving!" Another of the ruffians leveled his rifle toward Kate.

The ambient light from the headlights silhouetted her attackers but did not penetrate into the woods to make her visible. She could see the barrel of the gun lining up with her body. Kate didn't have time to move out of the way. Her shotgun was perched on another dead branch and aimed at the hooligan. She let her left hand slide down to the trigger. She squeezed.

Kaboom!

"Ahhh! They shot me!" The man's arm was bloodied. He dropped his rifle.

"Where are they? How many of them are there?" The driver ducked behind the front bumper of the bucket truck.

"In them bushes! Down low!" shouted the injured man.

The driver took two more pot shots with his pistol. One bullet hit the dead limb on which Kate had tripped. He fired three more rounds.

"Get a flashlight!" yelled the driver.

Kate gently crawled to the base of a massive pine, putting her back against the trunk for cover.

POW! POW!

The potshots continued. She racked another shell into the chamber during the gunfire so the aggressors wouldn't hear.

"Go on, Chet! Get into the woods with that light." The driver gave instructions to the other man.

"How about I hold the light and you go first?" Chet replied.

"I bet it's that girl who was driving that little car. You afraid of a little girl, Chet?"

"She killed Dave, same as a man would've. I'll hold the light," Chet insisted.

"Fine!" The leaves crushed under the foot of the driver when he stepped into the brush. "Chicken."

Kate knew she had to take out Chet with the flashlight. As long as they couldn't see her, she still had a chance. She watched the beam of the flashlight bounce around from tree to tree. She pictured in her mind about where Chet would have to be for the light to hit the distinct locations.

"I thought I saw something," the injured man yelled. "Steady your light over to the left, about three feet."

Kate knew that would put Chet's light right on her tree. She spun around and raised the shotgun.

BOOOOM!

The flashlight dropped, but the shotgun's muzzle flash had given away her position.

The driver's pistol spat out a barrage of bullets. Kate ducked behind the pine.

She heard the driver's pistol click.

"Kenny, give me some cover fire. I'm gonna

reload, get Chet's light, and kill this little witch."

Kate couldn't let that happen. She popped up from behind the tree and fired at the driver who was putting in a fresh magazine. POW!

The driver fell to the ground. Kenny, however, was still on the move. The injured man quickly collected the driver's pistol with his good hand. He ran to the front of the Escalade. "I'll kill the driver. He's still alive. You can save him. Put your weapon down and come on out. If I hear that pump rack another shell, he's finished."

Kate could do nothing. She was trapped. She believed the part about him shooting Terry if she racked another round. But what if she put down the gun and came out? He'd kill Terry anyway, just as he'd planned to do before. She had to think of a way out. She whispered to herself, "He's bleeding bad. I just need to stall until he passes out."

Kate readied her hand on the pump to reload in an instant and called out to Kenny. "Forgive me for not taking you at your word. If I come out, you'll kill me and you'll shoot the man in the car anyway. Why don't you just leave?"

The injured man replied, "No ma'am. I got your friend here at point blank range with my pistol. If I get more than a few feet away, I lose my leverage."

"We're in sort of a stalemate then," Kate yelled.

"Not really," said Kenny.

"Oh yeah?" Kate fished a shell out of her jeans pocket and fed it into the tubular magazine as silently as possible.

"The way I see it, you care about these people in this vehicle. Otherwise, you'd have kept on driving.

I've been shot. I'm a desperate man with not much else to lose. Either you put down the shotgun and come on out, or I'll kill 'em."

She placed another shell in, using the man's voice for noise cover. "If you kill them, you can bet I'll finish you off."

"If I don't get out of here and get some help, I'll die anyway. So, like I said, you're the one who stands to lose in this situation. And my patience is about to run out. I'll count to ten, then either you come out, or I'll kill your friends here."

Kate hated the ultimatum. She clenched her jaw. "Wait a second. I think we can work this out to where we both get what we want. Why don't you get in the truck and drive away?"

"So now you expect me to trust that you'll let me leave. Nope, not gonna happen. I'm done talking. One. Two. Three. Four. Five."

Kate swallowed hard. The pressure of the event felt like a vise on her head. She could not let this man kill Terry. But she could not surrender.

"Six. Seven. Eight. You just come on out." The man paused.

Kate had no alternatives. She'd simply have to try to beat him to the draw. "Impossible. He's right there. As soon as I rack the pump, Terry's dead. And I'll spend the rest of my life knowing that I sealed his fate."

"Time's up, missy. Nine. Ten!"

Bang!

Kate heard the pistol snap and spun around from the back of the tree, simultaneously, she racked the next shell into the chamber and leveled the bead sight toward the man. But he wasn't there. Kate traversed the woods, careful not to trip again. She emerged from the tree line and hustled to the front of the Escalade. Kenny was slumped against the front wheel well—dead.

"Aunt Kate."

She spun around to see Sam holding Chet's pistol in his hand. "Sam! Are you okay?"

He rushed toward her. "Yeah, how's Mom and Dad?"

Kate smashed the rear window of the Escalade with the butt of the shotgun and opened the back door. "Terry!"

Her brother's voice was hollow. "My seatbelt. It won't unbuckle."

Sam said, "I have a knife."

Vicky soon arrived. "Mom?"

"She's unresponsive," Terry said.

Kate reached up front and felt Penny's neck. She had no pulse and was already getting cool. She slid out of the way to let Sam work on cutting the seatbelt to free Terry.

Once Terry was free, Sam said, "We've gotta get Mom out. Will her seat belt release?"

Kate pressed the button on the buckle and the seatbelt fell away. She didn't have the heart to tell Sam that his mother was gone.

"Mom, wake up!" Sam pulled her lifeless body to the back seat. "Mom!"

Vicky looked on in horror. "Is she breathing?"

Sam continued to yell. "Mom! Mama, wake up!"

Terry was in pain but crawled through to inspect his wife. He tenderly pulled the hair out of her face.

His expression showed that he knew she was gone.

"Mom." Vicky's sobs showed that she too realized that Penny was no longer with them.

Sam began trying to give her mouth-to-mouth, then tried chest compressions, talking to her as if his pleas might bring her back.

Powerless, Kate looked on, wishing she could change the circumstances, wishing she could comfort her family.

CHAPTER 16

Behold, the Lord maketh the earth empty, and maketh it waste, and turneth it upside down, and scattereth abroad the inhabitants thereof. And it shall be, as with the people, so with the priest; as with the servant, so with his master; as with the maid, so with her mistress; as with the buyer, so with the seller; as with the lender, so with the borrower; as with the taker of usury, so with the giver of usury to him. The land shall be utterly emptied, and utterly spoiled: for the Lord hath spoken this word. The earth mourneth and fadeth away, the world languisheth and fadeth away, the haughty people of the earth do languish. The earth also is defiled under the inhabitants thereof;

because they have transgressed the laws, changed the ordinance, broken the everlasting covenant. Therefore hath the curse devoured the earth, and they that dwell therein are desolate: therefore the inhabitants of the earth are burned, and few men left.

Isaiah 24:1-6

Kate inspected her brother who had a long gash topping the swollen knot on the left side of his forehead. "The vehicle rolled twice. You got knocked around pretty good. I'm guessing you have a concussion. Do you want to try to find a hospital?"

Terry wiped the blood from his forehead with the back of his hand. He stared at Penny laid out in the back seat. "No. I want to get my kids to the cabin where they'll be safe. Then, I want to get up in the morning and bury my wife."

Kate tenderly put her hand on Terry. "We should call 911."

Sam and Vicky held each other while they cried. Terry pulled his kids in for a hug and looked up at his sister. "The world is falling apart. The perpetrators are dead. There's nothing the police can do at this point except slow us down."

"I agree. But, if we get pulled over and questioned, we'll be in the wrong. At least let me call it in and report the incident. I'll say that we're in fear for our lives and that we have to continue to our destination. The police can come interview us at the cabin."

Terry rubbed the backs of Vicky and Sam's heads. "I guess that would be okay."

Kate pulled out her phone. She dialed 911. "All circuits are busy."

She hung up. "It won't go through. At least I have the call in my log so we can prove we tried to call. I'm going to collect the guns. Do you want to see if the Escalade will start?"

Terry kissed each of his children, then crawled past the corpse of his dead wife to get back in the vehicle.

Kate picked up the weapons. She retrieved a short-barreled revolver from the first man she'd killed and a compact 9mm from the driver. She wedged the 9mm in her waistband, then placed the rifle and the other pistol in the trunk of her Mini. Sam offered her the large-framed pistol he'd used to kill Kenny.

She looked at the heavy semi-automatic. "Maybe you should hang on to that until we get home."

With his head hung low in grief, Sam stuck the gun in his waistband.

Kate turned in the direction of the wrecked SUV, hearing a steady clicking sound, but no engine ignition. She walked up to the shattered back window and addressed her brother. "I don't think it's going anywhere."

Terry continued to turn the ignition. With each turn, the clicking sound grew more faint. "We need the SUV."

"We'll go in my car. Come on." She patted the side of the Escalade.

"How are we going to transport Penny's body and the four of us in a Mini?" His voice was filled with the frustration of a man who wanted to grieve but couldn't.

"I'll clear out the trunk. We'll put Penny in the back."

"What about our supplies? We need our supplies. The kids don't even have clothes at the cabin."

"We'll carry what we can in our laps. We'll get by, Terry."

He crawled out of the stalled vehicle. "What about the Georgia Power truck?"

"It's stolen. The last thing we need is to catch a grand theft auto charge."

Terry looked at the big work truck. "I'd rather take a chance with the truck than leaving our supplies behind. And there's no way I'm leaving Penny on the side of the road. I'll drive the truck."

"I don't think you should be driving. I'm almost certain you have a concussion. Why don't I drive the work truck and let Sam follow me in my Mini? Vicky can ride with me. You ride up front with Sam, and we'll lay Penny out in the back seat of the Mini."

Terry stared sorrowfully at his wife's body. "I guess that will have to work."

"Okay. I'll start unloading the supplies from the Escalade." Kate started toward the SUV.

"Kate?" Terry's voice cracked.

"Yeah?"

"If we don't have room, I suppose you can leave Penny's suitcases behind." His lip quivered, then he began to sob.

"We'll make room. The kids will want to go through her things. You might even want to put her in something nice." Kate looked the large service truck over. "We'll clear out those tool boxes. We can even put a few bags in the bucket."

Kate began reorganizing the storage compartments of the bucket truck and loading up the bags and supplies into every available space. She left Vicky, Sam, and Terry alone to grieve. She'd miss Penny. Even though Kate had tried, the two of them had never been close.

Before getting into the truck, Kate retrieved the short-barreled revolver from her trunk. She handed it to Terry. "Sam still has the pistol he used to bail us out."

He took the weapon and glanced at his son who was getting into the driver's seat. Terry appeared to be pained over Sam having to kill the man. "Okay."

"And here's your radio. Let me know if you see anyone coming up behind us." Kate passed him the walkie-talkie.

"I will."

Vicky stood by the back window of the Mini, staring at her mother's corpse in the back seat. Kate put her arm around her niece and gently pulled her away. "Come on. We need to go."

The rest of the trip to Waynesville was uneventful. The small towns they passed through had no gas stations open where they could refuel.

Each of the towns seemed to have turned off the welcome signs and all but rolled up the sidewalks to let everyone know they were closed for business. The two-vehicle convoy drove by several local sheriff's cars parked in groups of three or four. Several had their lights flashing but none of them gave Kate's group any trouble. They seemed to prefer that people keep on driving.

Kate dared not to breathe a sigh of relief when she turned onto the road where her father's old cabin was located. She slowed down before coming to the steep gravel driveway. She wanted to be sure she had the big work truck positioned right so she could increase her speed to make it up the hill. Once she felt confident, she gunned the accelerator. The heavy tires spit gravel as the vehicle climbed up the drive. Kate stopped short when she saw a car in the driveway.

Quickly, she put the truck in park and killed the engine. "Vicky, stay down!"

Vicky complied.

Kate called over the radio. "Terry, someone is here. Have Sam cut the ignition. Hopefully, they didn't hear us."

"I see 'em. Do you know anyone who drives a busted-up '97 BMW?"

"No one I know," Kate replied. "Get that rifle out of my trunk and come up to the work truck. We'll use this vehicle for cover."

Terry's voice came over the radio. "Coming now."

Kate quietly opened the door. She passed the revolver to Vicky. "If you get into trouble, point and shoot."

"I will." Vicky held the gun awkwardly.

Kate gave her a nod of confidence, grabbed the shotgun, then exited the cab. She peered around the front bumper, watching the cabin.

"See anything?" Terry arrived carrying the rifle.

"No."

"Look, a woman just walked past the window." Sam stood behind his father with the large pistol in his hand.

"I told you to wait in the car!" Terry spoke louder than he should have.

"Dad, I've already killed someone. I think I'm qualified to be here."

"Get down! Be quiet." Kate motioned for them to lay low. "I think the woman spotted us. Get ready in case they come out shooting. We have to take our cabin back, no matter what."

Terry looked at his son with regretful eyes. "Stay back. You can cover us from behind the truck."

"Okay," Sam conceded.

The front door of the cabin opened. Kate pressed the butt of the shotgun into her shoulder and got ready to engage.

"Who's out there?" yelled a man.

Kate peeked around the front bumper of the service truck. "Boyd?"

"Kate? Is that you?"

She lowered her shotgun. "Boyd, who else is here?"

"My girlfriend, Tina. We decided to take your advice when everything started falling apart."

Kate came out from behind the work truck. "You

brought supplies?"

"No. I tried, but everything was closed or the lines were crazy. Are you guys okay?" Boyd walked down the stairs and hugged Kate.

"We had a rough trip." Terry shook his brother's hand.

Kate thought nothing of Boyd inviting his girlfriend without asking first. It was his typical modus operandi. She put her hand on his shoulder. "Help me get the supplies inside, and I'll tell you about it."

CHAPTER 17

As the door turneth upon his hinges, so doth the slothful upon his bed. The slothful hideth his hand in his bosom; it grieveth him to bring it again to his mouth.

Proverbs 26:14-15

Early Wednesday morning, Kate stuck the tip of the spade shovel into the earth and pressed it down with her foot. "I didn't want to say anything in front of Tina, but you should have asked before you brought her. It's bad enough that you showed up empty-handed, but bringing another mouth to feed was not cool."

Leaning on the handle of the flat-edged transfer shovel, Boyd took a long draw from his cigarette. "I couldn't just leave her behind. And like I said, I tried to get supplies."

"If you had tried when I called you, you'd have had no problem." She loosened the dirt and scooped it to the side.

Boyd stepped back as if he didn't want to get dirt on his shoes. "You didn't really give me any details. You have to admit, the story sounded kinda kooky until it actually happened."

"Well, now we have limited resources. So you and Tina are going to have to earn your keep if you expect us to feed you."

"Not really—the resources, I mean."

"Explain." Kate's forehead puckered. She continued to dig.

"You've got a lot of stuff. Especially with all that extra food we hauled in last night. And with Penny being gone, the numbers sort of even out."

"Show some respect!"

"Chill out, I'm just saying."

Kate jabbed the shovel into the ground. "Who says we were planning on you showing up empty-handed?"

"Weren't you? I mean, come on. This is me we're talking about. The loser black sheep brother." His tone was sarcastic.

"I'll feed you. But you're going to have to work for it. Tina too."

"Yeah, sure. Whatever."

"In fact, you can start right now. Start digging."

"This is a flathead. I can't dig with a transfer shovel."

"Oh." Kate looked at Boyd as if he'd made a

valid argument. "Hey, I've got an idea. Let's trade." She handed him the spade and took the shovel Boyd was holding.

"How are you going to dig?" he asked.

"I'm not." Kate started walking back to the house. "I can't dig with a flat shovel."

"You expect me to dig a grave all by myself?"

"Six feet deep. Six feet long. Three feet wide. Let me know when you're finished. You can get started on making dinner."

"What about everybody else?" Boyd protested.

"Everybody else thought ahead and brought food. If you want to eat, you'll have to work for it. Every meal, Boyd."

"That's not fair. Don't treat me like the red-headed stepchild."

Kate fumed. She spun around. "No, Boyd. It's not fair. We made plans, bought provisions—risked life and limb bringing them up here. I warned you long before the 60 Minutes show about the attacks, yet you squandered your opportunity. However, I did notice you managed to get a case of vodka and three cartons of cigarettes. Everyone else in the country who didn't heed the warning is going to starve to death. But you, Mr. Golden Boy, get a second chance. Your family, who has put up with more of your garbage than anyone else, is willing to let you work for some of the precious food they set aside for their own survival while the rest of the country starves. So, you're right. It's not fair. It's not fair to me, to Terry, to Sam, or to Vicky. But once again, we get to reap the rewards of your bad behavior. So if you want to make things more equitable, feel free to take your booze, your cigarettes, and your girlfriend, and go home."

Boyd glared at her with a look of disdain. With a loud defiant grunt, he drove the shovel into the ground.

Kate turned and walked back toward the house. "And make sure Tina understands what will be expected of her. I shouldn't have to be the one to tell her."

Kate went to the master bedroom, which Terry would be using. Penny was laid out on the bed. Terry and the kids had dressed her in a clean outfit. They sat in chairs on the side of the bed.

Kate stood in the doorway with her arms crossed. "You guys doing okay?"

"As well as can be expected." With his arm around her back, Terry held Vicky's head to his chest.

Kate was at a complete loss for words. She felt like she didn't belong in the room, so she left. "I'm going to make a run into town. I want to see if anything is available at all. I'll be back soon."

"You can't go by yourself. Let us take the day to say goodbye to Penny. I'll say a few words, then we'll bury her this afternoon. I can go with you to town tomorrow," Terry said.

Kate looked at the time on her phone. "I'm sure the panic hasn't set in here like it has in Atlanta. But these people saw the news last night. They'll be lining up first thing this morning to get any supplies that are to be had. Delivery trucks won't be running. Whatever is on the shelves now is all there is. When it's gone, that's it."

Vicky and Sam looked at their father. Terry ran his fingertips along Penny's arm. "What are you going to try to get?"

"Gas, if there is any. We need bullets. We have guns, but the people who attacked us didn't have much extra ammo in the truck. And we could always use extra food, especially since Boyd brought his girlfriend."

"I really don't want you to go by yourself. And I'm sorry, Kate. I'm just not up for the ride right now." Terry's face was filled with pain.

"I'll take Tina."

"You don't even know her. Why don't you take Boyd?"

"He's working on the . . ." She glanced at her sister-in-law's corpse but couldn't bring herself to say the word.

Terry nodded that he understood.

Vicky commented, "I don't think Tina is awake yet."

"I'll go," Sam volunteered.

"No, Sam. Your sister and I need you here today."

"Aunt Kate needs me. And we all need the supplies. Besides, sitting here staring at Mom like this isn't helping me. Getting out of the house would be the best thing."

Terry seemed to not have the strength to argue. He pleaded with Kate. "If you see the slightest hint of trouble, come straight home. We don't need any of those things as much as we need you both to come home safe."

Kate replied, "I'll come right back if there's

trouble anywhere. No unnecessary risks, I promise."

Her statement seemed to put Terry at ease. "Okay, let me give you some cash."

"I have money. Keep yours for now."

Terry said, "Hurry back."

Vicky looked up. "Can you try to find some flowers? For mom?"

"I'll try sweetheart." Kate put her hand on Sam's shoulder. "Come on."

He followed her to the hall. "Are you bringing a gun?"

"Yeah. Do you have yours?"

"It's under my bed. Should I get it?"

"Yep. I've got some ammo for you. Let's top off your magazine before we go." Kate walked upstairs with Sam to get the pistol, then crossed the hall to her room and retrieved the extra bullets she'd found in the cab of the service truck. She kept them in a paper bag on the shelf in her closet. "I think these go to your gun." She handed a box of ammo to Sam.

".45, yep this is what I need."

"Oh, so you know about guns?"

"I know this is a .45." He released the magazine and began feeding bullets into the top.

"You seem fairly proficient with reloading."

"I couldn't sleep last night. I messed around with it until I figured out the basic mechanics."

Kate had done exactly the same thing with the 9mm when she couldn't fall asleep.

"I can keep the rest?" Sam held the half-empty box up.

"Sure."

He picked up another box and extracted a long shell. He read the label. ".270. Wow! What's this go to?"

"The rifle we picked up. I guess it's for deer."

"Or moose." Sam cracked a smile for the first time since his mother had died. "That's a big bullet."

"Yeah. I hope we never have to use it, but it's nice to know we have it if we do." She tucked the bag back on her shelf. "Let's get going. I want to get to the store before it opens."

The first stop was a shooting range and gun store called Mountain Range. Several people were lined up at the front door waiting for the shop to open. Kate hurried to get in the line before it grew. Minutes later, the door unlocked and a man stuck his head out. "Five people at a time."

Moans and murmurings erupted in the crowd.

The man said, "We're trying to accommodate everyone, but we're going to do this our way. If you don't like it, you're more than welcome to go to another store. We're going to run out of stock in a couple of hours anyway." He held the door open for five customers, then locked the door behind them.

Kate quickly did a head count of the people in front of her. "Nine people. Let me stand in front, and you come in with the next round if we can't go in together."

Sam did as she asked. "Okay."

They waited and minutes later, three people came out the door. Two were carrying long-gun cases and boxes of ammunition. The store clerk let three more people in to take their place, then locked the door.

"At least it's moving fast," Sam said.

Kate felt anxious. Minutes felt like hours. To her, it did not seem fast.

The next time the door opened, four people emerged, each was heavily laden with firearms and ammunition.

"I hope they still have something left when we get inside." Kate had no idea how large the store's inventory of ammo might be.

Finally, their turn came. Sam was allowed to go in with Kate. She hurried to the counter. "I'd like five hundred rounds of each of these calibers."

The man looked at the piece of paper she handed to him. "One thousand round limit per customer. But I might be able to make it easy for you. We sold out of 9mm ball last night. All I have is high-end hollow point; 20-round boxes at $20 bucks each. I doubt I have 500 rounds."

"Price isn't an issue. And my nephew is with me. Does he get a thousand rounds?"

The clerk replied, "Yep. But about the shotgun ammo, all I have are target loads. Will that be okay?"

"I guess it will have to be."

The clerk scratched his beard. "I'm not sure I have five hundred rounds of .270 either. Might have a couple hundred."

"Okay, give me whatever you have."

"Sure, just give me a minute." The clerk took the paper to the back with him.

Sam tugged Kate's sleeve. "Should we get some

holsters? And what about slings for the shotgun and the rifle?"

Kate turned to look at the gear that Sam was pointing to. "Maybe so. Go ahead and pick out anything you think will work for us. And see if they have any magazines that fit our 9mm or our .45."

The man returned. "I got 400 rounds of 9mm and 220 rounds of .270. You have 500 rounds of the .357, .45, and shotgun shells. It's a little over your combined quota of 2000 rounds."

"Thank you. I appreciate that," Kate said.

Sam placed the holsters, magazines, and slings on the counter and the man rang up the purchase. Kate paid him.

"You better bring up a cart. The shotgun shells alone weigh about fifty pounds."

Kate turned to see that Sam had already gone to retrieve a cart from the front. The items were loaded with haste and they made their way back to the car.

Jealous snarls watched them walk by with the goods. One man made a snide remark. "Hope you left some for the rest of us."

Kate didn't make eye contact with any of them but could feel the angry stares. "Let's get this stuff into the trunk and get out of here as soon as possible."

Sam helped her shuffle the boxes into the back of the Mini then pushed the cart out of the way. Seconds later, they were gone.

"Where to next?" Sam inquired.

CHAPTER 18

If a brother or sister be naked, and destitute of daily food, and one of you say unto them, Depart in peace, be ye warmed and filled; notwithstanding ye give them not those things which are needful to the body; what doth it profit? Even so faith, if it hath not works, is dead, being alone.

James 2:15-17

"I'd like to stop by Ingles. I bought all the rice and beans they had last time. Those are easy-to-store staples. It would be good if we could load up on a few more bags of each." Kate felt the trip had been worthwhile already because they'd picked up some ammo, and because Sam seemed distracted from his grief. She also wanted to grab some flowers while at the local chain grocer but didn't mention it to Sam. He needed no reminding of the sad task which lay before them once they returned home.

"Wow! Look at the parking lot. It's packed." Sam pointed at the melee in front of the grocery store. Horns beeped and drivers yelled at other motorists as they jockeyed for parking spaces.

Kate hesitated before turning into the lot. "We'll park at the far corner. It looks like tempers are on edge."

"People are lined up for gas too." Sam's gaze followed the line of cars stretched out along the road to access the fuel pumps.

Kate twisted her mouth to one side. "That's not good. I was hoping to fill up before we went home."

"You have half a tank. How much gas does your car hold?"

"Sixteen gallons or so. The service truck only has about a quarter tank remaining. I'm sure Tina and Boyd didn't bother to top off her tank when they came. If they did, it would be very uncharacteristic of Boyd." Kate parked in the field at the back of the parking area. She and Sam cautiously made their way to the entrance. Signs on the doors read *Cash Only*.

As they arrived, a young woman with two small children riding in a full cart came out the sliding doors.

A manager pursued her. "Ma'am! You haven't paid for your goods. You cannot leave." He grabbed the sleeve of her jacket.

She pulled away and kept walking.

"Ma'am, I won't let you leave." The manager rushed to the front of the cart and grabbed it forcefully. Soon, a clerk joined the manager in apprehending the woman.

The woman tried to push past them both, but they overpowered her. The children, a girl about four years old and a boy who looked to be less than two, began to cry. The mother joined her kids. Amidst her sobs, she said, "Then call the police. I can't just leave empty handed and watch my babies starve. All I have is credit cards and a bank card. I don't have cash."

The manager swallowed hard as if he were holding back tears himself. "I'm sure everything will be worked out in a day or two. But I can't let you take merchandise you haven't paid for."

Kate dug into her bag. She counted out three hundred dollars and approached the manager. "This should cover what she bought."

The manager looked at Kate with a look of uncertainty and confusion. He looked at the woman's cart as if he were considering whether or not to make her come in to ring up the food items. He nodded to the clerk who was still holding the front of the young mother's cart. "Let her go."

"Thank you." The woman dried her eyes and offered Kate a smile. "Thank you so much."

"No trouble at all." Kate felt horrible for the woman. She knew the cart full of food wouldn't last long, and that without help from others, the small family's odds of survival were slim.

Sam watched the woman proceed to her vehicle.

"That was a nice thing to do, Aunt Kate."

She put her hand on his shoulder. "If we lose our humanity, our survival is in vain."

Once inside, Kate grabbed a cart. The aisles were overflowing with shoppers and the shelves were sparsely stocked. "Look! Bread!" She took three loaves.

Sam examined one. "Sprouted bread? That sounds gross."

"It's good, trust me. The fact that people think it's gross is probably why it's still here. I'm sure the Wonder Bread sold out minutes after they opened the doors." Kate pushed the cart in search of anything else that might be of value.

Sam froze. "They have plenty of flowers."

"Do you want to pick some out? You know more about what she'd like than I would."

He nodded and walked slowly toward the floral department.

Kate stayed near, ready to comfort him if he broke down, but he did not. Sam kept a stiff upper lip and selected two beautiful bouquets.

Sam placed them in the cart. "Can we see if they have any strawberry Pop Tarts? Vicky would like those."

"Sure." Kate pushed the cart down the canned goods aisle. All the shelves were bare.

Sam picked up a few packages from the international food section. "Think these are like cookies?"

Kate read the label. "Digestives. I'm not sure, but they're the closest thing to a cookie we'll find today."

A woman hurried past Kate, bumping her with the corner of her cart. Kate ignored the offense and avoided making eye contact.

The next aisle over was cereal. It was bare except for a few containers of oatmeal and some boxes of single-serve grits. Kate loaded them into the cart. "Looks like someone beat us to the Pop Tarts."

Sam led the hunt for other edible items. "Look, Cupcakes, Zingers, and Twinkies!" He scooped up the synthetic treats like he'd struck gold.

Kate wrinkled her nose at the artificially-colored and artificially-flavored selection of sweets but said nothing to discourage her excited nephew. They had bigger problems than the likely carcinogenic effects of Red 40 and Yellow 6.

The next items on the shelves were vegan meat substitutes. "Here's some tofu hot dogs."

"No thanks." Sam waved his hands.

Kate tossed several packages into the cart anyway. "These are less gross to me than real hot dogs."

They navigated through the traffic jam of grocery carts to the next aisle.

"What about almond butter?" Sam held up a jar he found next to the empty shelf where the peanut butter had been.

"I've never tried it, but it sounds good. Load 'em up." Kate continued to the rice and beans aisle. It was empty as she suspected.

"Anything else?" Sam asked.

"Not that I can think of." Kate was all but certain she'd regret not buying more products in a few short weeks, however, her mind was spent and she simply couldn't think what else to get.

"Do we have laundry detergent?" Sam asked.

Kate stopped short. "No. At least not much. Soap, shampoo, deodorant, we'll need all of that stuff."

"Those shelves are nearly full." Sam led the way down the aisle and began loading up the cart.

A robust bearded man with less-than-stellar hygiene and a greasy camouflaged ball cap approached Kate's cart. "Bill, where are you?" The overweight man looked behind him, then focused on the contents of Kate's haul. "I think I found where all the bakery treats went."

He glared at Kate as if he were sizing her up for a confrontation. "If you eat all this junk food, you're liable to get bigger than me."

"That's none of your business." Sam quickly stepped up to Kate's side.

"Oh, I guess you're the one hoarding all the Twinkies. Someone ought to teach you some manners, share with others and that sort of thing. Since I'm here, I guess it'll have to be me. I'm going to take half of your snacks. Next time, be polite and leave a few for the next guy."

Sam shook his head. He attempted to reason with the oaf. "There's hardly anything left in the store. It's all we could find. I'm not trying to be a hog, but we have to have something to eat."

"It's okay, Sam. Let him take what he wants." Kate tugged Sam's arm.

The oily giant rummaged through the cart. "Best listen to your ma, or whoever she is."

Sam fumed. "My *ma* is dead, because of a bunch

of idiots who thought they could just take what they want. Idiots like you." Sam knocked the cakes out of the ogre's hand.

The man shoved Sam, knocking him to the floor. "How about I just take everything then? I was trying to play nice, but if you want to be a little punk . . ."

Still sitting on the floor, Sam lifted the back of his jacket and drew the pistol out of the holster in his waistband. "Walk away from our stuff or I'll kill you."

The man sniggered. "You ain't gonna kill nobody, boy."

"Let it go, Sam." Kate helped him up from the floor and attempted to take the gun.

In a rage, Sam jerked his arm away from her. "I'll blow your brains out."

"Give me that gun, you little runt." The dingy blob reached for Sam's pistol.

POW!

The enormous man lost his humorous expression. Shock filled his eyes. He covered his massive belly with his hands and toppled to the floor.

"What did you do?" Another man, with a similar hat, and similar standards of cleanliness grabbed Sam from behind, restraining his arms.

"Pete! Are you alright?" The man called out to the melted glob on the floor who was leaking bright red fluid.

Pete was not alright. Kate gritted her teeth and drew her pistol. "Let go of him!"

"No doin', lady. This boy's done shot Pete. He's fixin' to go to jail. Put that gun down, boy!" The second man was smaller than Pete, but still much larger than Sam, picking him up from the floor and shaking him.

"Your friend instigated this. He brought it on himself. Put the boy down, or I'll put you down!" Kate followed the man as he stepped from side to side twisting Sam in an effort to make him drop the pistol. Crowds of onlookers gathered at each end of the aisle.

"Put him down, please," Kate begged.

"Lady, I'll whoop your tail if you still have that thing pointed at me when I'm finished with the boy, here."

"I will kill you. Put him down. This is your last chance." Tears streamed from her eyes, making her look weak.

"You'll do no such thing. Now put that gun away before you hurt yourself."

Kate sobbed with remorse over what she had to do. But if she didn't, Sam didn't stand a chance.

Bang! The man's face exploded in a fantastic eruption of crimson. He fell to the floor, taking Sam with him.

"Come on, we have to go." Kate clutched Sam's wrist and pulled him up.

Sam gripped his pistol tightly with his right hand. With his left, he grabbed one of the bouquets of flowers before he sprinted out of the grocery store behind Kate.

Kate's feet pumped across the pavement and to her car in the far field. Once Sam was inside the vehicle, Kate stomped the accelerator and gunned the car out of the store's parking lot.

"I'm sorry, Aunt Kate. But I couldn't just let them bully us."

"It was just cupcakes, Sam."

"No, it wasn't just cupcakes. That's what they tell kids in school. But believe me, I've watched kids who just roll over. The torment doesn't end for them. Once they give in to one bully, they're marked. Every animal in the school will prey on them."

"This isn't high school, Sam." Kate blew through a yellow light, watching the rearview for signs that they were being chased by police.

"You're right. In high school, allowing bullies to win usually only costs you your self-respect and maybe your lunch money. Now we're in the real-life apocalypse. Here, the bullies kill you." He paused for a moment and looked at the bouquet of flowers. "Or worse, they kill your mom."

Kate felt terrible for the boy. He had a point, but she couldn't condone killing people in a supermarket over cupcakes. With her hands shaking against the steering wheel, Kate kept her eyes on the road.

CHAPTER 19

Without counsel, plans go awry, but in the multitude of counselors they are established.

Proverbs 15:22 NKJV

Every bone in Kate's body told her to go straight home. She'd promised Terry that she'd bring Sam back if there was the least sign of trouble, and they'd had trouble in spades. But she wasn't ready to explain to her brother what had happened. She wasn't really sure how to put it into words.

"Why are we turning here? Isn't the cabin the other way?"

"Yes, but I want to get off the road. We'll go sit by the lake for a little while and let things cool off."

Sam didn't argue. Kate parked in a wooded area by the lake. "Come on, we'll walk around for a few minutes. If we see trouble with the car, we can hike home on foot."

"Do we bring the guns?"

"From here on out, we always bring the guns." Kate closed her door softly so not to make too much noise.

They walked silently for a while. "Do you want to sit on a bench or keep walking?" she asked.

"I prefer to walk. I've got too much nervous energy to sit right now. I think my head would explode."

"That's about how I feel."

Roughly an hour later, Kate had heard no sirens or seen any indication that anyone was looking for them. "I guess we could head back."

"Okay." Sam followed her to the car.

Kate's situational awareness was maxed out. She looked carefully down every road for signs of police. Holding her breath, she turned back onto the main road and headed toward the cabin.

"Aunt Kate?"

"Yes?"

"I don't want to make you more nervous than you already are, but a police car just pulled in behind us."

The blood drained from her face. Her hands went cold and she had the sensation that she'd just walked off a cliff. She tried to swallow, but her throat and mouth were as dry as salted sand. She felt dizzy and had to remember to breathe. Kate forced herself to look into the rearview. The police car was feet away from her bumper. If they were looking for her car, she was minutes from being apprehended. If they weren't, she was perhaps seconds away from making a fatal mistake out of sheer fright.

Instinctively she turned off the main road. The patrol car followed her causing her heart to race even faster. She saw the red awning of Carolina Readiness ahead and hit her blinker indicating her turn. She had no chance of outrunning the police car nor his radio. If this was the end, she figured it was best to get it over with. She pulled into the only free parking space at the preparedness store.

The police car drove on by. Kate watched in terror, not daring to take a breath.

Sam turned around to monitor the patrol car's trajectory. "What is he doing?"

"I don't know."

"What are we going to do?"

"Go inside in case he comes back by."

Sam's face was pale with trepidation. "Okay."

Kate uneasily opened the door and stepped out of the vehicle.

Sam followed her in the store.

"That's gotta be the luckiest girl in the whole world." Bill stood near the counter with his hands on his hips.

How could he possibly know? Had he been one of the people in the crowd? Did Bill watch me and Sam gun those men down? What is he thinking? Is he going to turn me in? Her thoughts raced. Kate considered running for the door. She'd take her chances with the officer in the patrol car seeing her.

Sam, with his eyes as wide as bucket lids, seemed to be wondering the same thing. But unlike

Kate, he did not wonder in silence. "What—what do you mean?"

Bill laughed. He walked up to Kate and put his hand on her shoulder. "This girl waltzed into my store and wanted to know what kind of things she ought to buy to survive a catastrophic collapse of the banking system." Bill winked at Sam. "And would you believe not forty-eight hours later some fellow came on the television talking about Cyber Armageddon or some crazy thing. Well, lo and behold, I'd say that about sums up our present situation. That's on par with hitting five power balls in five different states all in the same week. Where I come from, we call that lucky."

Kate quickly realized Bill was not referring to the shooting and she began to breathe a little easier.

"You look a little tense. Relax. Remember, you're the luckiest girl in the world." Bill smiled. "Anything I can help you with?"

Kate looked around the store. Slowly, her heart rate began to stabilize. "Um, maybe. Do you have any more of that food like I bought?"

"No, ma'am. We sold out of that Monday morning after the 60 Minutes interview. As you can see, we've been busy. I was planning to close up shop at around 2:00 PM today. Not much left to sell. I doubt we'll open back up unless things normalize. But according to what the guy said, that's not likely to happen. Would you happen to know that fellow?"

Kate looked away and didn't answer. "What kinds of things do you still have in stock?"

Bill didn't push her for an answer about knowing

Albert. "If this turns out to be a prolonged event, no amount of food storage will get you through. You'll need to start producing your own food at some point. Do you have seeds?"

"No. But that makes sense."

"Let's get you set up with a good variety." Bill began plucking several packets of each kind of seed from his display. "In any given season, you'll have a bumper crop of something, some plants that do okay, and a few utter failures. Every year will be different. Make sure you sock away lots of seeds every year and always keep enough seed to have two more bad years. Do you know anything about gardening?"

"Not really."

"You probably need some books. Here's one on gardening, and another on general homesteading topics. You might want this one, too. It covers wild edibles in our area. How well are you stocked on medical supplies?"

"I . . . I don't know. I guess I didn't think of a lot of things. I figured if I had some food we'd be okay."

"Food is important. But there's more to it than just that." Bill led the way to the next row of shelves. "Let me know if I start worrying you about the budget."

"No. We have cash. I appreciate your recommendations." Kate signaled for Sam to get a cart. The items were piling up.

"I do have whole wheat berries. People don't buy them like they do the other heat-and-eat foods."

"Wheat berries?"

"Yes, they're the kernel, the whole grain. They'll keep forever as long as they stay in their natural state."

"How do you prepare them?"

"You can mill them into flour. Or you can boil them and eat them like oatmeal or put them in a salad."

Kate looked at the large buckets which had been overlooked by the masses, much like the tofu hotdogs. "How do you mill them?"

"We sell grain mills. You can use the mill for dried corn also, to make cornmeal."

"Cornmeal for cornbread?" Sam asked.

"Sure," Bill answered.

Kate looked at the seeds in her cart. She saw two different varieties of corn. She'd neglected to think about the long-term process of survival. "I'll take a mill and some wheat. How much do you have?"

"I have a pallet of wheat. How much can you carry?"

"Maybe ten buckets. And I'll take one of those hand-held Ham radios you told me about."

"Okay, let's get you settled up." Bill made his way to the register. "If I were you, I'd hit the local big box home improvement store before they close down for good. I'd pick up several bags of salt, like they use for water softener systems. I'd also get some chicken wire. You'll probably want to get chickens and rabbits at some point. Meat is going to be hard to come by."

Kate counted out her money.

Bill helped them load up the car.

"Where is Jan?" Kate asked.

"She's minding the fort. Folks know we're pretty well set for a situation like this. If they thought no one was at the house, some who failed to take the advice we've so generously dispensed over the years might decide to help themselves to our supplies. She's there to keep honest folks honest."

"Please tell her I said *hi.*"

"I'll do that." Bill pulled out a business card and jotted down a set of numbers on the back. "Tune into this frequency every afternoon at 3:00. It's a communications network of people like us. You'll be able to stay abreast of what's happening around town. You'll be able to connect with us if you decide that's something you'd like to do later on."

Kate looked at the card. "Thank you."

"Now remember, that's our little secret."

"Absolutely. Thanks again for everything." Kate got in the car.

Sam did likewise. "Are we going to the home improvement store now?"

"No. We don't even have room for anything now. We at least have to go home and unload. I'd rather take Tina's car *if* we decide to go back out." Kate remembered the cruel job awaiting their return. "Maybe we'll do that tomorrow. We can focus on saying goodbye to your mom for the rest of the day."

Sam's voice was solemn. "I'd rather honor her memory by making sure we have the things we need to take care of Dad and Vicky. That's what would be important to her."

"Okay, we'll see when we get home." Kate was impressed by her nephew's strength. But she hoped he wasn't cheating himself out of his necessary time to grieve.

CHAPTER 20

Rejoice with them that do rejoice, and weep with them that weep.

Romans 12:15

The family stood around the grave site. Kate scowled at Boyd. She could smell the vodka on his breath. Penny's body had been wrapped tightly in crisp, clean, white sheets. Terry and Sam held opposite ends of the same rope which supported Penny's upper torso, while Kate and Boyd held the rope holding the lower portion. The two teams slowly lowered Penny into her final resting place.

Tina tried to hold Vicky's hand, but the young girl refused to let the stranger comfort her. Once the corpse reached the bottom of the grave, Kate pulled the rope out from beneath and coiled it up. She placed it on the ground and went to her niece's side.

Boyd looked at the pile of dirt he'd excavated. "Terry, do you want to say a few words before we…?"

Terry stared blankly into the open pit in the ground. "I don't know what to say."

"Dad's Bible is in the cabin. Should I get it?" Kate asked.

Terry shook his head. "I wouldn't even know what to read."

"Someone is coming." Tina signaled with her eyes toward the house on the next lot.

All the homes in Apple Blossom Acres were on 2-to-6 acre lots. Kate could see the person coming toward them was an older man but could not make out his face.

"It's Harold Pritchard. He and Dad got to be friends over the years." Terry's face was listless.

"I don't think I ever met him." Kate watched the man approaching.

"He keeps to himself. Kind of a curmudgeon." Terry replied.

As the man came near, Kate could see he was toting a Bible. His hair and beard were white and his pants and jacket were black. She could not tell if his face was in a frown, or it was simply the lines of age about his eyes and forehead which gave him the appearance of one less than pleased with the general state of affairs.

"You the McCarthy boy ain't ya?"

"Yes, sir," Terry answered. "Mr. Pritchard, is that correct?"

The old man looked over the crowd before

nodding at Kate. "And you're the girl."

Kate forced a smile at the unflattering salutation.

"I'm their brother, Boyd." He stepped forward and offered his hand.

Pritchard did not accept the greeting. "Yeah, I heard all about you."

Boyd scoffed and withdrew his offer of a handshake. "Whatever."

Terry looked at the grave. "Is there something we can help you with, Mr. Pritchard? We're mourning our loss right now."

The old man crossed his hands with the Bible over his stomach. "Thought I'd offer to read a Psalm, ask a prayer for your comfort if you desire. Your pa was a right good man."

"Are you some kind of a preacher?" Boyd shook his head in annoyance.

Pritchard coughed out a laugh. "No. I'm no kind of preacher. At least not the kind most churches would have. Most of 'em's got no tolerance for the truth. Better part of 'em's little more than country clubs with no liquor. Well, I guess some of 'em's got liquor by now. But I know the Word." He nodded confidently.

Terry answered. "I'd appreciate that, Mr. Pritchard. My wife," he paused. "Sam and Vicky's mother, we lost her on the way out of the city. Things are bad in Atlanta."

Harold Pritchard opened his Bible. "Unto thee, O Lord, do I lift up my soul. O my God, I trust in thee: let me not be ashamed, let not mine enemies triumph over me. Yea, let none that wait on thee be ashamed: let them be ashamed which transgress without cause. Shew me thy ways, O Lord; teach me thy paths. Lead me in thy truth, and teach me: for thou art the God of my salvation; on thee do I wait all the day. Remember, O Lord, thy tender mercies and thy lovingkindnesses; for they have been ever of old. Remember not the sins of my youth, nor my transgressions: according to thy mercy remember thou me for thy goodness' sake, O Lord. Good and upright is the Lord: therefore will he teach sinners in the way. The meek will he guide in judgment: and the meek will he teach his way.

All the paths of the Lord are mercy and truth unto such as keep his covenant and his testimonies. For thy name's sake, O Lord, pardon mine iniquity; for it is great. What man is he that feareth the Lord? Him shall he teach in the way that he shall choose. His soul shall dwell at ease; and his seed shall inherit the earth. The secret of the Lord is with them that fear him; and he will shew them his covenant. Mine eyes are ever toward the Lord; for he shall pluck my feet out of the net. Turn thee unto me, and have mercy upon me; for I am desolate and afflicted. The troubles of my heart are enlarged: O bring thou me out of my distresses. Look upon mine affliction and my pain; and forgive all my sins."

Pritchard closed the Bible and bowed his head. "Lord comfort these children with your Holy Spirit. And as David has pleaded in this Psalm, forgive our sins, though they be many."

Kate stood with her eyes closed and her head bowed. She waited for the man to finish. Several seconds passed and he was silent. She peeked with one eye to make sure he was still praying. She saw that he'd already cleared several yards on the way back to his home. She looked on curiously.

"Weird, huh?" Boyd commented.

"Creepy," Tina added.

"It was a kind gesture, even if his social graces are less than refined." Kate pulled Vicky close to her.

Terry nodded in agreement. His face showed his inner agony. He picked up the shovel to toss a scoop of dirt into the pit. He paused as if the task were too much for him to handle emotionally.

"Boyd and I will finish up." Kate took the shovel.

Terry took several labored breaths and headed back to the house.

Vicky put her arm around her father and her head on his shoulder. "Are you coming, Sam?"

"Soon." Sam took the shovel from Kate. "I want to be the one to do it."

Kate relinquished the tool. "Okay. But I'll be right here if you want me to take over."

On the following morning, Kate and Sam headed out to see what other supplies they could secure. Their first stop was the local big-box home improvement store. When they arrived, other customers were in the store loading up on various items which might increase one's odds of survival.

Kate took a flatbed cart. "Sam, you get a regular cart. And if someone gives us grief about wanting what we have, just let them have it. I'm not going to risk my life over anything in this store."

"Okay." Sam huffed to show his disagreement.

"Should we get some gas cans? Fuel is already in short supply."

Kate stopped short. "Good call. I didn't even think of that." She scanned the aisle labels suspended high above the end caps like street signs. "This way."

They reached the aisle where gas cans had once been, but the shelves were empty. "We're too late. What else could we put gas in?"

Sam shrugged and looked around.

Kate's eyes scanned the aisle. "Come on. Let's get that fencing material and the salt before it's all gone."

Sam followed close. "Grandpa left a bunch of tools in the garage, right? Do we have hammers, nails, screwdrivers, that sort of thing?"

"I haven't inventoried it, but yeah, we've got a big box of tools down there." Kate loaded a roll of chicken wire and a roll of welded-wire fencing onto the cart. Then, Sam assisted her in stacking forty green metal fence posts neatly onto the flatbed cart.

Kate paused to look at a stack of five-gallon utility buckets. "What about those? Think we could fill them with gas?"

"Then how would you get the gas into the tank?" Sam inquired.

"I'm sure we'll figure something out. I'll dip it out of the bucket and into a funnel with a coffee cup if I have to. The most important thing is getting gas while we still can." Kate examined a stack of lids for the buckets.

"How many should we get?" Sam grabbed a pile and placed them on the flatbed cart.

"Let's get ten."

"I think you'll incite a riot at the gas station if you try to fill up ten buckets full of gas."

"You're probably right. I'll only fill two at a time."

"Five trips to the gas station? Good luck with that. The lines are at least half an hour long. You'll be all day. That is if there's even any gas left by the time we get out of here."

"It will be our next stop." Kate wheeled the cart to the aisle where the salt was located.

Sam commented while standing in line, "I'm surprised how many of the people around here still use cash."

Kate replied, "It's keeping the local economy going while the big cities are completely shut down. But I'm afraid it won't last long."

After checking out, they loaded the supplies into the back of the Mini, then tried to find a gas station which was still open.

"There's one!" Sam pointed at the long line of cars in queue for fuel.

She quickly changed lanes and joined the column of vehicles. Kate sighed at the thought of the arduous wait ahead. They inched forward and Kate wondered how much gas she was burning. She glanced over at her nephew. The inactivity was giving him time to miss his mother as evidenced by the sullen expression on his face. "Your father is very proud of you. And I'm sure Vicky is very grateful for all you are doing for them. Your mom would be happy to know that you're stepping up."

Sam turned to give Kate a contrived smile then,

without speaking, turned to gaze glumly out the window once more.

Rather than force conversation, Kate purposed to let Sam grieve a while in silence. He needed it.

Finally, they reached the pump. "Sam, can you go pay?" Kate passed him a fifty-dollar bill.

Sam headed inside, and Kate got out to pump the gas. When she saw Sam leave the register, she began topping off her tank. Next, she pumped gas into one of the five-gallon buckets. Once filled, she signaled for Sam to place the lid on it while she moved to the next bucket.

The man in the vehicle behind her got out of his car. "Hey! What is this? You can't put gas in buckets!"

She replied politely, "It's for our truck. I wasn't sure it had enough gas to keep running while we waited in line."

"I don't care what it's for. You can't be hogging all the gas!" He signaled to the people in line behind him. "Are you all seeing this?"

Soon, more people got out of their cars. "Come on, lady!" Another man said.

"Leave some for the rest of us!" a woman yelled.

"Cap it off," Kate put the pump handle back into its receptacle.

"We still have ten more dollars on the pump!" Sam protested.

"Doesn't matter. Put the lid on and let's go."

Sam snapped the lid on the second bucket which was nearly full.

Kate could see the snarl growing on Sam's face. "Come on, get in the car."

Sam seemed reluctant to comply but did so anyway.

Kate sped out of the station.

"We can't let people bully us, Aunt Kate."

"We're not, but we're not going to get into a gunfight every time someone says a cross word to us. You've killed two people in two days. Your father doesn't even know about the grocery store or I'm sure he wouldn't have let you come today."

"You've killed more people than I have."

"That's not the point. Everyone is on edge, and they're allowing themselves to become animals. I don't want to stand idly by and watch that happen to you. We'll do what we have to do when we have to do it, but when we have the opportunity to walk away, we're going to take it."

Minutes later, Kate traversed the crooked little road up the mountainside to the cabin. Once there, she and Sam began to unload the supplies into the garage.

Sam hoisted one of the buckets of gasoline in the door of the garage. "I hear a vehicle coming up the road."

Kate closed the garage door. "Let's make sure they aren't coming here. I don't want to advertise what we have."

A silver Subaru Outback pulled into the drive and the woman behind the steering wheel cut the ignition. Kate closed the hatch of her Mini.

A woman in her early sixties exited the Subaru. She carried a black folder, wore a burnt-orange long dress and flat-bottomed, open-toed shoes.

Kate's curiosity bordered on confusion. She

watched the woman fight to traverse the steep gravel drive in an attire that would have seemed out of place even in the best of times. And these were anything but the best of times.

"Hello, you must be the McCarthys."

Kate fought to hide her bewilderment. With a half-smile, she said, "Yes, I'm Kate. This is my nephew, Sam."

Terry walked out onto the porch but did not introduce himself.

The woman looked at him long enough to allow him the opportunity to give his name, however, he did not. With a nervous and tightly-wound grin, she said, "I'm Edith Ramsey, the president of the Apple Blossom Acres homeowner's association. It's a pleasure to meet you. I've brought a copy of the covenants and restrictions for your review. There have been some complaints. It seems you've had a work truck parked on the property, which is in violation of your agreement."

Edith looked into the back of Kate's car. "Is that livestock fencing?"

"Um, I suppose it could be." Kate took the black folder and opened it.

"Well, just as a courtesy, I'll remind you that livestock isn't allowed in Apple Blossom Acres."

Kate's brows slid nearer one another. "You mean like cows and pigs?"

"Anything. Rabbits, chickens, goats." Her face contorted into a rigid saccharine smile.

"Mr. Pritchard has chickens." Sam looked to the rickety old coop next door.

Edith's expression soured, her mouth wrinkling

like a prune. "Harold's coop was here prior to the covenants being adopted. It's grandfathered in."

"The country is melting into chaos, Mrs. Ramsey. It's hard to say how long it might last. Maybe we should consider relaxing the rules." Kate tried to sound polite.

"Who complained?" Terry glared down from the porch with his arms crossed.

"That's not important. What is important is that we maintain our community standards." She turned to Kate. "And the country may very well be melting down, Ms. McCarthy. All the more reason for the neighborhood to be stalwart in keeping our goals toward excellence."

Terry cut in again. "Only four other houses are further up than our cabin, and one of those is Mr. Pritchard's. I can't imagine that he complained. Maybe it was just some busybody who has nothing more to do than concern themselves with how other people live their lives."

"This is a vacation home to you. I wouldn't expect that you'd have the same level of commitment as those of us who live here year-round. Nevertheless, if the truck is still there tomorrow morning, the board will be forced to levy a fine against your property."

Kate interjected in an attempt to bring the civility back to the conversation. "Wouldn't it be better if the HOA suspended the restrictions until the crisis has passed? We left Atlanta and it was frightening. I think if the residents had an idea of what was going on, they might want to come together to make sure we all have food, water, and security. People are dying out there. Don't think because Apple Blossom Acres is tucked away in the hills that we're all immune from the mayhem. Maybe we could call a special meeting and the board could vote on relaxing some of the restrictions that could get in the way of our survival."

"I think you're overreacting because of what you've seen in Atlanta. That's understandable, but there will be no special board meetings, and you'll abide by the covenants. Good day, Ms. McCarthy." Edith turned toward her vehicle.

"I'll take it upon myself to see if there's any interest among the residents in forming a block watch or a community garden." Kate stood adamantly with her hands on her hips.

Edith whipped around with her finger pointed. "You'll do no such thing. Polling residents is an official HOA duty."

"Oh, nothing formal. Just me being neighborly. I'm sure there's nothing in the covenants against that."

"It could be interpreted as soliciting. That's a finable offense." Edith Ramsey stomped off to her Subaru.

"Then fine me!" The volume in Kate's voice rose in defiance.

"Good job, Sis." Terry was almost grinning. But sorrow quickly returned to his face and he went back inside the house.

Kate hated the situation. She looked between the tall tree trunks to see Harold Pritchard standing on his porch, observing the commotion. He was too far away to tell for sure, but Kate thought for a moment that the old curmudgeon might actually be chuckling at the scene. She muttered to herself, "I'll start with him in canvassing the HOA for allies. I'm sure he's no fan of the restrictions. He'll know who will be sympathetic to our cause."

CHAPTER 21

As it is written: "There is none righteous, no, not one."

Romans 3:10

Friday morning, Kate walked outside onto the porch to find an empty bottle of vodka and an ashtray full of cigarette butts. Several more butts were strewn about the yard in the vicinity of the front porch. She gritted her teeth. "I knew this was going to be a problem. I guess no one gets to pick their family. You get the hand you're dealt and you have to make the most of it."

She was determined not to let this annoyance divert her from her mission. Kate marched across the most sparsely wooded section of the lot to Pritchard's four-acre lot. She knocked on the door and waited. No answer came, so she knocked again. She felt nervous approaching a stranger's house. They'd met and were neighbors, but she knew nothing about the man other than the fact that he was peculiar, so to her, he was still a stranger.

After waiting for what seemed like minutes, Kate felt awkward and wanted to leave. But the task at hand was important. Forming alliances in this new, hostile world could literally be the difference in life and death. Terry would be much better at this sort of thing, but it could be weeks before he felt up to socializing. Sam and Vicky were too young. And Boyd, well, he was Boyd.

Kate took a deep breath and knocked again, this time more firmly.

Minutes later, Harold Pritchard came to the door. "What is it?"

"Mr. Pritchard, hi. I wanted to invite you over for coffee. If I'm not interrupting anything, of course." Her smile quivered with anxiety.

"I was trying to watch the news. And I've already had coffee."

Kate wanted to dismiss herself but held fast. "Oh, the news. It's terrible isn't it?"

"I wouldn't know. I'm not watching it right now." He began to close the door.

"I made cheese biscuits." She felt ridiculous immediately after issuing her desperate plea.

Yet it caused Harold Pritchard to pause before slamming the door in her face. "Cheese biscuits?"

"Yeah, I mix shredded cheddar in the dough."

"What kind of cheddar?"

"Um, Kraft, I think."

"No, girl. I mean sharp, mild, what kind?"

"Extra sharp."

"Why don't you fetch them biscuits and come over here. You can watch the news with me if you like. I've got half a pot of coffee."

"Okay then." As quirky as the invitation was, Kate considered it a win. "I'll be right back."

She hurried back to the house to find Boyd and Tina sitting down at the table with bloodshot eyes, coffee, and a plate full of cheese biscuits. She snatched up the biscuits. "Make your own food…" She carried the plate with her. "After you clean up the mess on the porch and the cigarette butts in the yard."

Kate rushed back to Mr. Pritchard's door and rapped gently.

"Come on in the house," he called.

Kate made her way to the living room where the elderly man sat in front of an old tube television set. The news portrayed footage of riots in Seattle.

"They're a burnin' down their own houses. It'd be one thing if they had somewheres else to go, but they ain't."

"I'm glad we're far away from all that." Kate placed the biscuits on the coffee table.

Pritchard shook his head. "Asheville ain't but thirty miles from here."

"Asheville is quite a bit smaller than Seattle, or Atlanta where we're from."

"It's big enough if all them hippies and junkies come this way. Lord knows we don't need any more of 'em than we done got." Pritchard picked up a biscuit and bit into it.

"I haven't seen that many around here—people who look like drug addicts at least."

"Oh, we got 'em. The half backs is bad enough."

"What's a half back?"

"Folk like that Edith Ramsey you got into it with yesterday. She moved from Boston down to Flardy, then up here. Gets too hot for 'em and they move to the North Carolina Mountains. They move halfway back up north; half backs."

"Oh. What about people like us who just come up once in a while? What do people call us?"

"Tourists." Pritchard polished off the biscuit.

Kate twisted her mouth to one side. "Is that better than being a half back?"

"Naw it ain't. It's worse. But I liked your pa. So you get a pass."

"Oh, thanks, I guess."

"What'd you do to get Edith all stirred up?" He seemed to be fighting a grin.

"She doesn't like that bucket truck parked in our drive."

"She don't like a lot of things."

"You mean like your chickens?"

His eyes were still glued to the television. "Like my chickens. Tell you the truth, I get tired of foolin' with 'em. But I don't like nobody telling me what I can and can't do on my own property."

"Then why did you move to an HOA?"

Pritchard got up from the well-worn couch and made his way to the kitchen. "Wasn't like this when we moved here. Years ago, we had a dairy farm outside of Charlotte. Some big developer fella came along and offered me a deal I couldn't refuse. Me and the wife had always wanted to live in the mountains, so we took the money and came up here. The HOA didn't do nothin' in them days except maintain the road. We all paid our fair share for the upkeep and it was just fine."

"So what happened?"

"Half backs happened. Makin' rules about how big a house had to be, no trailers, no junk cars and all that. Sounds fine and dandy at the beginning, but once the camel gets its nose under the tent, it wants to begin tellin' you what color britches to wear." The old man returned with two cups of coffee. He placed one in front of Kate.

"Thank you." She sipped the stout brew and puckered at the bitterness. "Where's your wife?"

"She went on home to Glory six years ago. Left me here to wallow in this confounded mess alone."

"I'm sorry."

"It's the way of the world, consequence of the original sin. It's appointed unto man once to die and after that, the judgment.

"I'm awful sorry for them youngins. Don't seem right them losin' their ma at that age. They'll be lookin' to you for nurture. Especially the girl. She'll be needin' someone to coach her into womanhood."

Kate listened. She thought about the curious choice of words Pritchard had used at Penny's funeral. Despite his backwoods nature, Mr. Pritchard seemed wise. "What you said over my sister-in-law's grave, about our sins being many. Why did you say that? I mean, you don't really know us. We're basically good people."

Pritchard tittered. "Ma'am, ain't nobody good

but God. Scripture says so. Ever last one of us has broken God's law, time and time again. You tellin' me ain't none of ya ever told no fib?"

"Well everybody does that."

"And what does that make 'em?"

"Liars, I guess."

"Ain't never took nothin'? Not in your whole life?"

"Maybe like a piece of gum. I never killed anyone, and I never robbed a bank."

"But you've just admitted to being a lying thief. According to God's standard, you're a sinner."

"I go to church."

"Your church don't tell you that lying thieves go to hell?"

"They don't talk about that kind of stuff." Kate felt defensive. "But you're not perfect either."

"Never claimed to be. I'm just washed in the blood of Jesus. I try to live a life worthy of the sacrifice He made, but I fall miserably short. I need grace every day.

"But churches not tellin' folks that there's consequence to sin is why we're in the mess we're in."

"What mess?"

"This!" Pritchard motioned toward the dusty television screen.

"What, you think this is some kind of judgment from God?"

"I know it is. I'm just surprised He's given us as long as He has. I've been expecting something like this for decades."

Kate shook her head. "I don't think God had

anything to do with this. People are dying. God is patient and kind."

"Yes, He is, but He is also righteous and just. You ever read the Bible cover to cover?"

"No, I don't think I'd be able to understand it."

"That's hogwash—exactly what the Devil wants you to think. You'd understand it just fine. If'n you hit a spot that don't make no sense, you just pray. God will reveal it to you... most of it anyhow. Some of it I still don't understand, but I get the main gist of it. The rest, well I reckon God will reveal to me when I get to Glory Land.

"You read it through, especially the books of prophecy. See if none of it don't sound familiar about the way folks is behavin'; especially toward God. And see if none of these catastrophes don't ring a bell, too."

"Yeah, okay. I'll try."

"Don't try. Either do it or don't do it."

Kate looked down. The old man had struck a nerve. She wasn't sure how accurate his appraisal of the situation was, but she intended to find her father's Bible and see if it was true. "The reason I had come over here was to ask if you'd be interested in working together to keep an eye on things in case conditions continue to deteriorate. Also, I wanted to ask if you'd like to work on a garden together and perhaps be willing to give us some pointers on raising chickens. If so, I thought you might know if anyone else in the community had a similar mindset about those things."

Pritchard said, "You want to get folks movin' before Edith poisons their minds and talks them into sticking their heads in the sand."

"I suppose that's another way of putting it, yes."

"Alright, girly. Count me in." He slapped her knee, then took another biscuit.

CHAPTER 22

He who walks with wise men will be wise, but the companion of fools will be destroyed.

Proverbs 13:20

One week passed. The cities around the country continued to melt into anarchy and pandemonium. One by one, the stores in and around Waynesville shuttered their doors due to a lack of goods to sell.

Likewise, one after the other, the cable news channels went off the air. All were located in major cities which deteriorated from unsafe to uninhabitable.

Kate worked alongside Terry, Sam, Vicky, and Harold Pritchard in the garden behind the cabin.

Pritchard pointed to Sam. "Run on over to my

place and see if you can't scratch up a little more chicken manure from the hen house."

Sam pressed his lips together and glared at his sister. "Vicky, come on. Give me a hand with this."

Using the metal rake, she continued to bust up the large clods of dirt left by the tiller. "He told you to do it."

Terry stepped up and took the rake. "Go help your brother."

"But Dad, it's gross!"

"It's called survival, Vicky. Come on, please. Do it for me." He looked at her tenderly.

"Okay." Unenthusiastically, she trailed off behind her brother.

Kate sprinkled a few beet seeds into the ground and patted the dirt over them. "Boyd and Tina should have been finished cleaning up the breakfast dishes by now."

"I'm kind of enjoying being away from them for now. I don't mind working the garden." Terry's voice still had not regained its usual pep and vigor that it had possessed prior to Penny's passing.

Kate heard the sound of wheels crunching over the gravel drive. "Visitors." She pulled her shirt up over the small Smith and Wesson 9mm, which she kept on her at all times.

Kate stood to her feet and began walking toward the cabin. Terry and Mr. Pritchard followed her.

Pritchard spoke harshly to the uninvited caller. "Edith, what are you come to pester us about now? I done told you to write me all the fines you want."

"They are already written up. I'm just waiting for mail service to resume so I can send them via certified mail in keeping with HOA standards of notification." She stepped out of the Subaru wearing slightly more practical clothing than before.

Pritchard cackled. "Your own bureaucracy has gotten in the way of your bureaucracy. Woman, why didn't you just carry the letter down here with you?"

"I'm not here to argue, Harold. I'm here to issue a final warning. The Smiths, the Coopers, the Petersons, and I are leaving. We'll be going down to the FEMA relief center in Greenville, South Carolina. While we're gone, consider yourselves warned that there is to be no trespassing on any of our properties, for any reason. Additionally, there is to be no animal husbandry nor agricultural endeavors on any of the common areas, vacant lots, and especially on any of the plots where the owners are not here. While your blatant disregard for the covenants on your own property is merely a finable offense, I'll have you locked up for trespassing if it happens anywhere else."

"Very well." Pritchard turned his back to the snarling woman and made his way back toward the garden. "If I see any ne'er-do-wells snooping around your house, I'll just let them be; so as I'm not trespassing by shooing them off."

"For your sakes, I hope this is resolved quickly. You'll never make a garden at this time of the year. And once the relief centers are filled, they turn people away." Edith returned to her vehicle and slammed her door. The Subaru kicked gravel as she hurried out of the drive.

Kate caught up with the old man. "That makes

about half the community who have vacated their homes."

"Yep. The bad half. Good riddance to 'em. We won't never see them again."

"You think not?" she asked.

"They'll be dead inside of a week. The government ain't got the wherewithal to feed all them people."

Kate felt concerned about what Edith had said. "Is she right? Will we be able to get a crop to grow this late in the year?"

"We'll get a few things. Ever little bit will help. If the Lord blesses us and holds off the first frost a mite longer, that could make a big difference. But beets, cabbage, carrots, peas, they should all make somethin'.

"Mrs. Peterson used to make apple butter and sell it at the festivals. I bet she's got a canner and a good stock of Mason jars. We'll run down there and see in the mornin'."

Kate stopped in her tracks. "We can't break in and steal her stuff! They just left!"

"It's just borrowin'. We'll buy her some new ones when Edith gets to Washington and get this all sorted out. Besides, Mrs. Peterson won't need it. They won't be back. Otherwise, we'll just let someone else get it. We're their neighbors. Seems right and proper that we should be the ones to have it."

Kate tried but failed to adopt his logic. Nevertheless, she capitulated. "Someone who makes apple butter sounds like the type of person who would stick it out. I'm surprised she's going to the FEMA camp."

"Her nor her husband neither one can't think for themselves. Edith told them it was the right thing to do, so they did it."

"I told them that staying and working together was the right thing to do," Kate countered.

"They see Edith as an authority figure."

"And I'm just a tourist."

"'Fraid so." Pritchard bent down and began mixing small sprinkles of the chicken manure into the soil with a hand-held cultivator.

Sam returned toting an old galvanized pail. Vicky was right behind him with a rabbit. "We caught a rabbit in the trap!"

Sam handed the pail to Mr. Pritchard. "I think that's the last of it."

The old man took the pail. "Them hens'll make more. That's one thing they're good at."

Vicky showed the rabbit to her father. "Couldn't we keep just one?"

He pulled her tight. "I'm sorry, honey. You know what they're for."

Pritchard looked up. "Bring me that hare."

Reluctantly, Vicky passed him the animal. He took it by the ears and gruffly flipped it upside down. "It's a buck. We need one good buck. If I let you keep him alive to breed, will you promise there'll be no more pets?"

With excited expectation, she said, "I promise."

"Alright then. Put him in the cage and do what you like with him."

"Thank you! I'll be right back." Vicky skipped off to the cabin.

She returned minutes later and resumed gardening with the others.

"Is your lazy uncle sleeping?" Kate inquired.

"No. He and Tina are down in the garage with some guys."

Kate immediately stood up. She tossed her gardening gloves on the ground and stomped toward the house. Terry quickly caught up and shot out in front of her.

Kate arrived a second after her brother. Two scraggly-looking men were retrieving a bottle of whiskey and a carton of cigarettes from a backpack.

"What's going on?" Terry asked.

"We're just making a little trade. I'll explain it later. Wait for me upstairs." Boyd waived dismissively to Terry.

"No! No way! Boyd, you have absolutely nothing to trade with." Terry took the whiskey and the cigarettes and handed them back to the man with the pack. "I'm sorry he wasted your time."

"No can do, Cochise," the other man said. "We came all the way up here. We're not leaving without something. I don't want to get into a family squabble, but I need to get paid."

The man with the bag said, "We could make an exception. We'll settle for a twenty percent restocking fee."

Infuriated over the situation, Kate drew her pistol. "Or you could settle for me letting you walk away with your lives."

The first man shook his head and backed toward the door. "You're making a big mistake, missy."

"By letting you live? Is that a threat? Are you

telling me I should gun you down right here and now?" She gripped the pistol tightly.

"Aunt Kate? What's going on?" Vicky stood behind her.

"Nothing sweetie. Go back with your brother." She motioned with her gun. "You two, beat it. I don't want to see you in this subdivision ever again."

The two ruffians backed slowly out of the open garage, wearing menacing expressions as they left.

"I can't believe you!" Terry yelled. "What were you thinking?"

Boyd stood stubbornly. "I was thinking we have way more than enough and a bucket or two of this food wouldn't matter much."

"Well, it does matter!" Kate exclaimed. "You still have booze and cigarettes."

"We're getting low on smokes, actually," Tina said.

"I was talking to my brother. You're a guest; an uninvited one I might add, so you'd do well to stay out of this conversation." Kate turned back to Boyd. "I can't believe you brought them to our home, showed them everything we've got. You've endangered us all, your niece, your nephew."

Terry put his hands on his hips. "Boyd, you and Tina need to pack your bags. We'll give you a month's worth of food, but you have to go. Be gone by sunset."

"And go where? This is Dad's cabin. You can't kick me out!"

"You sold me your share because you wanted nothing to do with it. I absolutely can kick you out."

Terry stepped closer as if he were ready for the conflict to escalate to a physical level.

"Kate?" Boyd stepped back. "You have a say here. Are you going to let him kick me out? If you do, you're signing my death warrant. Can you live with that?"

Kate grunted and holstered her weapon. She exhaled angrily through flared nostrils. She crossed her arms tightly and pondered the conundrum. She glanced at Terry.

He turned to walk out of the room and flipped his hands in the air. "Do what you want. It's your call."

Kate glared at Boyd and Tina. "If you stay, both of you quit smoking and drinking as of right now."

Tina again spoke up. "Couldn't we taper off instead of going cold turkey? We've still got six bottles of vodka and five packs of smokes."

"No. I'm taking that. It's just been brought to my attention how valuable such commodities are. We'll use them to trade for something we really need."

Boyd stuck his hands in his pockets and tilted his head to one side. "I don't think that's really fair."

"Then pack up your cigarettes, your booze, and the rest of your belongings and be gone by sundown." Kate turned to leave.

"Okay, okay. We'll do it."

"Fine. Bring them to me right now." She spun back around.

With heads hung low, Boyd and Tina went upstairs to collect their sacred idols. Moments later they returned.

"Here." Boyd handed her a cardboard box.

Kate inspected the contents. "Four bottles, three

packs of cigarettes. You're holding out on me. Cough it all up or hit the road."

Boyd nodded for Tina to go collect the rest of the loot. Once she'd left the room, he said, "I was wrong to barter with the food without asking, but you really should have let it play out."

"And why is that, Boyd?"

He shook his head. "These guys are bad news. It's not just the two of them either. They run around with some pretty rough hombres."

"Boyd! What have you gotten us into?" Kate felt the anxiety building. She set the box at her feet.

He put his hands up. "Hey! I'm willing to accept my portion of the blame, but you're the one who made me break the code of conduct with these guys."

"No! Don't try to lay the blame on me!" Kate punched his chest with her finger. "You broke the code of conduct of being a civilized family member by allowing roughnecks like that around our house! Then to show them our stockpile; that was unconscionable." She let out a sigh of disgust and stormed off.

CHAPTER 23

Thy word is a lamp unto my feet, and a light unto my path.

Psalm 119:105

Kate watched the sunrise over the mountain from the upstairs window in her room. A light knock came to her door. She tucked the .270 hunting rifle behind the long curtain on the side of her window. "Come in."

Terry walked in. "Hey, did I wake you?"

"No."

"Did you sleep at all last night?"

"No," she confessed.

"Why? What's going on?"

She shook her head. "Boyd mentioned that these guys he was making the deal with are part of a larger consortium of hooligans. I was worried they might show up unannounced."

"Why didn't you say something? I would have helped you keep watch. We could have taken turns."

"I don't know. I feel like you already disagree with my call to let him stay. I suppose I'm second guessing the decision myself." She slumped over on the pillow.

"He's our brother. Deep down, I love him, too. But I worry that his toxicity is going to poison the well. Still, I let you have the final word and I support your verdict."

"The damage is already done. If these guys try to pull anything, we need to be ready for them." She closed her eyes for a moment.

"Okay, we'll put a plan together. I doubt they'd hit us in broad daylight, but I'll keep my eyes peeled. You get some rest for now. We'll talk about it when you wake up."

Kate sat up on the bed, her heart pounding. She looked around and finally got her bearings. "I must have dozed off." She looked out the window. The sun was low over the mountains to the west. She picked up the pistol from her nightstand and tucked it in her holster. Kate rushed downstairs to find Terry, Vicky, and Sam eating at the table. "Hey, where's Boyd and Tina?"

Vicky stirred some of her canned chicken into the rice and beans on her plate. "Eating in Boyd's room. Said they feel like being alone."

Kate looked at Terry who shrugged. Kate put her

hands on Sam's shoulder. "Uncle Boyd and his friend have decided to quit drinking and smoking. They might be a little edgy for a couple weeks. It would be best if we let them have their space."

Kate headed to the door.

"Where are you going?" Terry let his fork rest on the plate.

"The garage. I just need to check on something. I'll be right back." Kate hurried down and inspected the stockpile. Everything seemed to be in order, but she didn't trust her brother, and she certainly didn't trust Tina. She double checked the hiding place where she'd stashed Boyd's cigarettes and alcohol, making sure all the seals were still intact. Once she was satisfied that nothing had been disturbed, she headed back up to the table to have dinner with her family.

Terry looked at the kids. "Your aunt and I have decided that we need to start taking some precautions to make sure we all stay safe."

"Why? What's going on?" Vicky asked.

"Nothing is going on, but folks around the country are getting desperate. We need to put some safeguards in our routine, just in case." Terry nodded affirmatively.

"Is this because of those guys who Uncle Boyd was dealing with? Are they drug dealers?" Vicky asked.

"They may have been the catalyst to start the conversation, but we don't have any reason to believe that they're a threat."

Kate understood that her brother didn't want to frighten Vicky, but if she'd have asked Kate, there'd have been no soft-pedaling the explanation. She ate her food and didn't interfere.

"I found Dad's old whistle." Terry held up a stainless-steel whistle dangling from a piece of black cord. "The designated watch person can blow the whistle if there's danger."

"Then what? We all report to our battle stations?" Sam asked.

Terry looked at Kate. "For lack of better terminology, yeah, I guess so."

"Which would be where?" Vicky inquired.

"I recommend my room," Kate said. "I have a good vantage point over the property, plus the only way to get in is to come up the stairs. It's a natural kill zone that funnels our enemy right into our line of fire."

"Whoa! When did you start talking about funneling people into a kill zone?" Vicky laughed.

"She's a gamer, dork." Sam continued eating.

"I thought you played like Pokémon and stuff." Vicky took a piece of cornbread and broke off a corner.

"I would have," Kate sipped her water, "If Pokémon was a multiplayer first-person shooter," she said with a wink.

Vicky placed her cornbread on the plate. "Speaking of video games, what happened to the guy you used to play online with?"

Kate glared at Terry. "The one your dad wasn't supposed to tell anyone about?"

"Yeah, him." Vicky laughed.

Kate sighed. "It's a different world now. We rarely have an internet connection. When we do, it's too slow for gaming. Besides, there's no time for video games."

"I was asking about the guy, not the games."

Kate looked at the old wooden table, then glanced up at her inquisitive niece. "There's no time for boys either."

"Oh, we make time for boys!"

Terry perked up. "What boys are we making time for?"

"She flirts with the kid at the bottom of the hill." Sam forked a bite of rice into his mouth.

Vicky slapped his arm. "Shut up, I do not!"

Terry looked at Kate. "If you want to take first watch tonight, I'll relieve you at four o'clock."

"Are you sure you'll get enough rest?" Kate asked.

"Yeah. I'm going to turn in right after dinner." He looked at his kids. "And guys, everyone stays in the house until tomorrow morning. If you hear the whistle, no matter what you're doing, drop it and run to Aunt Kate's room."

"Everyone has a gun except me," Vicky said.

Terry looked at her remorsefully. "I'll protect you."

"What if you can't?" she asked.

Kate could see the heartbreak on her brother's face as he considered the reality of what Vicky was saying.

Terry looked down. "If you feel like you're ready, I'll walk you through operating the revolver and the rifle tomorrow."

"What if something happens tonight?" Vicky quizzed.

Kate put her hand on her niece's shoulder. "I'll show you how to use my 9mm after dinner."

"So, can I carry it with me?"

"I keep it at my side, but it will be in my room if you need it."

"You have two guns and I have none," Vicky said matter-of-factly.

Kate hated the thought of carting the shotgun around everywhere she went, but Vicky had a right to self-defense as well. "Okay. You can carry the 9mm."

Sam entered the conversation. "We need more guns. And more ammo."

Kate looked at her brother. She couldn't deny the truth in Sam's statement, but options were slim, and they needed more of a lot of things. "Yeah, and I wish I had something besides target load for the shotgun, like slugs or buckshot."

"You can change the target loads into something like an exploding slug, you know." Sam took a sip of water. "They'd be better than a slug."

Kate was befuddled by the statement. "They're target load. Basically, a bunch of little BBs. You can't change a shotgun shell."

"Yes, you can." Sam broke off a piece of cornbread and stuck it in his mouth.

Kate waited for him to finish chewing. "So… are you going to explain?"

He took another drink of his water and said, "Open the top of the plastic shell and pour out the BBs. Then, you melt some crayons or candle wax. You mix the BBs in the hot wax and pour it back into the top of the shell. When it hardens, it essentially becomes a slug."

"Until you shoot it," Kate said.

"Exactly." Sam smiled. "The slug stays intact until it hits the target, then it shatters and the BBs fly apart like a fragmentation grenade."

Kate knew the devastation of a frag grenade from years of gaming. It was a highly effective tool in any game where it was available as a weapon. She thought about the physics behind Sam's proposal. "Is this something you've tested out?"

"It better not be!" Terry interjected.

Sam shook his head. "Nope. But I saw it on YouTube."

"You better hope the hot wax doesn't set off the gunpowder in the shotgun shell." Vicky's statement inspired a new sense of respect for the manufacturing process that Kate hadn't yet considered.

Kate looked at her nephew. "The people on YouTube who were making these things, did they mention accidental discharges?"

"No, but we'll probably want to wear eye protection when we make them." Sam finished off his cornbread.

Terry blew out a deep breath. "If we decide to make these, your aunt and I will handle the fabrication process."

"It was my idea," Sam objected.

"And it was a good one. But I'm the dad, and I'm still calling the shots."

Kate heard a gentle rap on the front door. "I'll go see who it is." She peeked out the window to see Mr. Pritchard standing on the porch with an empty box.

She opened the door. "Mr. Pritchard. We were just having dinner. Would you like to come in?"

"Ain't got no time for that. Get yer shoes on and come on."

"Where are we going?"

"Down to the Petersons'. We need to get them jars."

Kate did not want to go. "Right now? In broad daylight? People will see us."

"It's nearly dark. Gets any darker and we'll have to use flashlights. That'll draw a heap more attention. Now quit yer fussin' and come on."

Kate gritted her teeth. "Okay, give me a second." She grabbed her hiking boots and called out to Terry and the kids, "I have to help Mr. Pritchard with something. I'll be right back."

"Hurry it up, girl." Pritchard headed down the stairs.

She pulled the back of her boot up and hopped along behind him. "My name is Kate, in case you forgot."

"I know what your name is, now come on!"

"Are you sure this is the morally correct thing to do?"

"What's the Good Book say?"

She tried to think of a passage that might apply to this situation while struggling to get her boots tied and keep up with the cantankerous old man. "Um, God helps those who help themselves?"

"No, girl! That ain't even in the Bible. I thought you said you went to church?"

"We went, but not every Sunday."

"How often did ya go?"

"Whenever, Christmas, Easter..."

"Just as well I reckon. You ain't never read the Bible, so you wouldn't know a good church if it slapped you upside the head anyhow. Goin' to church these days is about like pickin' mushrooms in the forest. If you try to do it without readin' the guide first, 'bout the best you can hope fer is a bad case of the scours. But you're liable to wind up dead.

"Naw, you can't be out rootin' around for a good church based on which'n has the best country club amenities. Best just go to the lake on Sunday and fish all mornin'. Least you won't be no worse off."

Kate's brow wrinkled at the bizarre reasoning. She wondered if her new companion might be a few cards shy of a full deck. "Is that what you do? You go fishing on Sunday?"

"Heavens no. I go to church. The one I attend ain't perfect, but it's the best one I could find; I looked long and hard to find it. Don't usually have much choice in politicians neither, but I vote; try to pick the one with the thinnest coat of muck on him."

Pritchard laughed. They rounded the corner going down the narrow asphalt road. "I reckon if I did find the perfect church I wouldn't go there no how."

"Why is that?"

"Wouldn't be perfect no more if I was to set foot in it."

Kate considered his answer. "You never told me what the Bible said about us breaking into our neighbor's house and taking her jars."

"It ain't breakin' in. We're lettin' ourselves in to collect her valuables for safe keepin'. If we take it, it'll still be hers when she gets back. And we'll return ever bit of it in as good or better condition as it was when she left. If'n somebody else was to haul it off, that be the last she'd ever see of it."

"You still didn't answer my question."

"The golden rule." Pritchard started up the Petersons' drive.

"Do unto others as you'd have them do unto you?" She followed behind him cautiously.

"Yes, child. If I was to suspend the good sense the Lord gave me and follow that fool woman off to a government internment camp, I hope someone would take pity on me and look after my things." Pritchard walked onto the porch and began looking under flower pots and beneath the welcome mat.

"It's very convenient that we're going to watch over only those items which serve to benefit us."

"Well, you haul the rest of their belongings all up to your house for safe keepin'. Me, I ain't got room for all of it. Ain't got a young back like yours for movin' a bunch of stuff up a hill neither. But you go right on ahead. Don't let me get in your way." Pritchard motioned for her to follow him. "Must a hid the key around back."

Kate saw the futility in arguing with the man so she trailed behind him. "Are you sure they keep a key hidden?"

"Everybody keeps a key hidden 'round these parts." Pritchard opened the side gate and walked through a well-manicured backyard. He lifted the top to the barbecue grill. "There it is." He retrieved a single key and let the top down on the grill. He shoved it into the deadbolt of the back door and unlocked it. He opened the door and let himself in.

Kate took a deep breath before going in behind him. Once inside she looked around.

Pritchard looked in the fridge first. Then he rummaged through the pantry. "Boy, their cupboards were as bare as a baby's bottom. I reckon they didn't have much choice but to go."

Kate thought about the food she'd stored. Perhaps she could have shared with the Petersons and they could have stayed. She quickly dismissed the notion. They had enough to get through the winter, and perhaps she could help Mr. Pritchard out, but if things didn't turn around soon, her family would be forced to abide by strict rations.

"Here's her jars. And would you believe, two cases of Mrs. Peterson's famous apple butter?"

Kate's eyes lit up, but she felt bad taking food from someone who had nothing. "I don't think we should eat the one thing they have."

"I might have a few things put away. If they come back, they'll want something besides apple butter. I'd have traded with them, if I'd have known." The old man stacked the empty jars, canning lids, and cases of apple butter by the door. "Best have a look around and see if anything else might need to be put away for safe keepin'."

Kate followed him into the bedroom and watched him pull open the nightstand drawer. He pulled out a small revolver.

"Little ol' .22. Wouldn't want that to fall into the

wrong hands. Speakin' of the wrong hands, sounded like quite the squabble over there with your brother and his compadres." Pritchard tucked the pistol into his belt.

"We asked his associates to leave and not come back. Making award-winning decisions has never been on Boyd's list of accomplishments."

The old man grunted. "Must be a box of ammo around here somewhere. Have a look under the bed, and I'll check the closets."

Kate peeked beneath the bed skirt. She saw a rifle case. "I think he has another gun under here."

"Pull it up. Let's see what you found."

She placed the plastic case on the bed and opened the tabs. "Looks like a shotgun."

Pritchard ran his fingers over the stock. "Walnut. Semi-automatic. That's a heap better weapon than what I've got."

"What do you have?"

"I've got an old double barrel shotgun and my grandpappy's old Colt Navy that he carried in the war."

"World War II?"

"No, girl. The Civil War. He was in the 37th Regiment, North Carolina Infantry. They fought at Second Manassas, Fredericksburg, Chancellorsville, he took a bullet in the arm at Gettysburg."

"Is it a dependable weapon?" She knitted her brows together.

"Yes, ma'am. I fire it off ever New Year's. Clean it real good and reload it. It's black powder, though. Takes a while to reload, so whatever you're gonna do, you need to get it done in six shots."

Pritchard continued to search the closet. "I bet we'll find us a .38 if we keep looking."

"Why do you say that?"

The old man placed several boxes of shotgun shells, twenty-two caliber ammo, and three boxes of .38 special bullets on the bed. "Just a guess." He motioned toward the dresser. "Have a look in that chiffonier."

"Why me?"

"Mrs. Peterson might keep her unmentionables in there. Wouldn't be proper me a rootin' through it."

Kate thought none of this behavior was proper but did as she'd been asked. Sure enough, Mrs. Peterson's underwear drawer had a very heavy object nestled beneath her bras. Kate carefully drew the snub nose revolver out of the dresser. "I wonder why they didn't take this with them?"

"Ain't no government camp gonna let you bring no gun. You can't have one in a library, a post office, nor a courthouse; you know good and well they won't allow you to carry one in the FEMA cage. Besides all that, Edith probably wouldn't have no one travel with her if they had a pistol. That woman would rather share a house with a polecat than have a gun around her."

"I've known a few people like that." Kate offered the pistol to the old man.

"How about your house? I see you packin' that pistol around like you're Annie Oakley, but do your folks have anything else?"

"We have a shotgun, a deer rifle, and three pistols."

"You go ahead and hang on to that .38. I'll keep

watch of these other two, if you don't mind."

"Yeah, sure." Kate tucked the .38 in her waistband. "Did you see any holsters in the closet?"

Mr. Pritchard took another look. "Nope. But look here what I found. A New King James Bible. It ain't no Authorized Version but I reckon it'll do for someone that don't go to church 'cept Christmas and Easter. I doubt Edith wants her travelin' companions to have one of these neither. Seems folk who don't like guns usually ain't got no time for the Good Book. Them devils at FEMA might not let 'em bring it in anyhow. How 'bout you hang on to that, too?"

She took the Bible. "Thanks. Are we finished? I'd like to get back home." Kate had done her share of burglarizing for the evening and wanted to get away from the crime scene.

"I reckon. Grab one of them boxes of apple butter and the empty jars. I'll haul the rest." Mr. Pritchard meticulously collected the ammo and guns and arranged them in such a way as to be able to carry them up the hill.

CHAPTER 24

And it shall come to pass, that whosoever shall call on the name of the Lord shall be delivered: for in mount Zion and in Jerusalem shall be deliverance, as the Lord hath said, and in the remnant whom the Lord shall call.

Joel 2:32

On Sunday morning, Kate awoke to the sound of someone banging on a metal pan. The sound was not only annoying and hyper-obnoxious, but it scared her half to death. She sprung from her bed and grabbed the shotgun. Her hands shook and her pulse throbbed. She fought to put her jeans on with one hand while she held the gun with the other.

Once they were on, she shuffled down the stairs with the barrel of the gun pointed at the floor. "What's going on?"

Boyd stood outside his bedroom door assessing the threat. "I think it's your geriatric boyfriend beating on a cook pot with a wooden spoon. He's hollering something about church."

The explanation made no sense to Kate so she proceeded to the front door. Carefully she peeked outside.

Terry was walking toward Harold Pritchard with his hands up. The old man ceased from banging on the pot and Kate could hear the conversation.

"We's fixin' to have church. I've got no bell, and I've got no steeple. Figured this'd be the best way to let folk know it's time to worship."

Terry dropped his hands. "I'm sure everyone on the mountain has heard the alarm. But I'm afraid you'll drive them off rather than attract them to your service. I'm sure you've heard the old saying you catch more flies with honey."

Pritchard looked over Terry's shoulder at the gaggle of neighbors coming up the hill. "Yep, I've heard it. But the fool who made it up ain't never been no dairy farmer. Ain't nothin' in the world attracts flies like cow manure."

Kate was wide awake and while she was still tired having slept only five hours, she was determined to go to Mr. Pritchard's church service…or whatever it was.

Kate hustled back upstairs, quickly washed her face, and put on a clean shirt. She grabbed the Bible which the old man had entrusted to her to keep until the Petersons' return.

Kate knocked on Vicky's door, which was across the hall from hers.

"Yeah?"

"Hey, it's Aunt Kate. Mr. Pritchard is having church. Do you want to come?"

"Yeah, there's nothing else to do." Vicky opened her door and came out wearing a ball cap and a comfortable sweater. She accompanied Kate to the door and stopped in her tracks. She put her hand over her mouth. "I've got to go change, fix my hair!"

Kate looked down the gravel drive to see the family from the bottom of the hill walking past to Mr. Pritchard's. Their very-good-looking son appeared to be about sixteen. She pressed her lips together. "Is that who Sam was talking about at the table yesterday evening?"

"I don't know. I'm just not going to church with a ball cap on, even if it's in some old man's backyard." Vicky raced up the stairs.

"Okay, I'll see you over there." Kate laughed.

She stopped by Boyd's room. "Hey, you guys going?"

"It ain't Christmas, and it ain't Easter. I'm not going to church." Boyd looked perturbed by the request and shut his door.

"Just thought I'd ask." Kate headed out the door.

"Wait for us," Terry called out. Sam followed close behind him.

"Is that Dad's old Bible?" Terry asked when he caught up with her.

Kate glanced down at the book, unsure how

ready she was to explain what she'd gotten into the prior evening with the self-appointed preacher next door. "Um, no. Mr. Pritchard lent it to me."

"Oh, that was kind of him."

"Yeah." She wanted to explain that it was no skin off his hide, but didn't.

When they arrived at their next-door neighbor's backyard, Kate saw twenty or so, thick, round logs standing up on their ends, like stools arranged around the trunk of a towering oak tree. They'd come from Mr. Pritchard's pile of firewood, which still needed to be split. Each one standing at roughly two feet tall, and more or less level, they seemed to have been divinely appointed for their makeshift purpose as church seating. "Wow. Look at that. The logs almost look planned. It actually looks like a chapel."

Sam added, "And most of the seats are already taken. We better hurry and claim our spots."

"Save a seat for you sister," Kate said to Sam, who rushed off ahead.

In one of the rare moments she shared alone with Terry, she hugged him as they walked. "How are you holding up?"

His eyes were pained. "I'm trying to be strong...for the kids. But I think I could use a trip to church."

"Well, I think you're doing a bang-up job. And I guess times being what they are, we could all use a trip to church."

Mr. Pritchard hurriedly handed out hand-written song sheets. "I've only had time to make up six of these, so some of you'ns is gonna have to share."

Kate smiled at the thoughtfulness of the gesture and would make a point of offering to type and print some for the following week. All of the stumps were filled with a few people sitting in the newly fallen leaves beneath the giant oak. She whispered to Terry, "This must be roughly half of the remaining residents in Apple Blossom Acres."

Terry looked around. "Yeah. If nothing else, it will be a good opportunity to meet the neighbors."

Kate looked back at Vicky who'd performed a miraculous five-minute makeover and was headed their way. "I think your daughter would second that opinion."

Terry seemed to miss the joke but waved at Vicky and signaled to her saved seat.

Pritchard, whose voice would win no awards in a competition, led the group in three traditional hymns. Afterward, he offered a short prayer, then opened a large, well-worn, leather-bound, Bible. He spoke from behind yet another section of a log. This one was roughly two feet in diameter and stood four feet tall. Unlike the others, it had a pitch on the top, which made it the perfect podium.

Pritchard looked out at his little congregation. "After 9/11 lots of folks made their way to church who hadn't been in quite a spell. I reckon some of you ain't been in some time. Others of you might go ever week. Maybe you're like me and can't get to your regular place of worship; bein's how there ain't much gas left.

"Anyhow, I welcome you all in the name of the Lord." He gave an abbreviated nod, similar to what country folks give to someone they pass on the road.

"I ain't never professed to be no preacher, so if'n any of youns feel led by the Spirit to speak, holler at me after church, and we'll talk it over. Even more so, I ain't never been accused of bein' no choir leader. So I pray, for all our sakes, that one of you'd step forward to handle the music; although I'll tell you right now that I ain't got much tolerance for none of that foolishness they play on the Christian radio." His brows furrowed, then softened.

"For those of you that ain't been going to church, you might find what I got to say this morning is a mite odd."

He paused and looked around. "Those of you who have been attending regular like, you're liable to find it downright insufferable. But keep in mind, ever word I speak is coming straight from the Word of God. So if you don't like it, don't shoot the messenger. Ain't my fault if your no-account pastors have been sellin' you a bill of goods and a false sense of security."

Kate tried not to laugh out loud. She found his willingness to offend absolutely amusing, particularly when she wasn't the only target of his galling oratory.

The old man cleared his throat and proceeded to read the entire first chapter of Joel. The chapter described in divine poetry, the plague of locusts which the Lord sent to lay waste the land of Israel.

Pritchard looked up from the text. "It'd be hard to ignore the similarities between the destruction brought about by the locusts here in the Good Book and what we've got goin' on here in this country.

"Some folk will tell you that all them Books of Prophecy only applied to ancient Israel and ain't got a thing to do with us today. But I'll remind them, between Ezekiel, Jeremiah, and Isaiah, just about every known kingdom of the day was prophesied against. Moab, Put, Cush, Babylon, Ethiopia, Assyria, Egypt, Tyre, Arabia, and a heap more that I can't remember just now.

"The Books of Prophecy ain't popular subjects in churches these days, despite the fact that a quarter of the books in the Bible are Books of Prophesy. And when a preacher does veer off the path of popular teachin', it's a rare thing that he'd point out the similarities between the sins of the ancient world and those of modern-day America—even more rare that he'd attempt to apply those warnin's to our country.

"So here we are. Having ignored the warnin's of God's Word, the locusts have done eat up all our money in the bank. And I know what you're thinkin', tweren't God who sent these locusts. It was some good-for-nothin over in Russia or China who's sent these devils upon us.

"Well, to that I'll say, 'cept the first tablets of the Law passed down to Moses, God didn't write one word in the Bible with His own hand. He used the hands of forty men, stretched out across millennia. Don't make it no less His doin', though.

"In Isaiah, God declares that He'd use Assyria to judge the northern Kingdom of Israel, and Babylon to judge the south. Don't make it no less His doin'.

"And while I could tell you more about the man in the moon than I could about how they came up with these confounded computer viruses, it don't make a hill of beans who done it. Might a been Russia, China, Kim Jong, or some little feller in his mama's basement right here in Waynesville; don't make it no less the Lord's doin.

"In Isaiah, the Good Lord lays out the crimes of Israel. He tells 'em they're rebellious, their rulers are corrupt and the companions of thieves, He blames them for killin' their babies, offering them up in sacrifice to Molech. He says they are filled with eastern ways, and have allowed the influence of the surrounding pagan culture to creep into their worship."

Pritchard paused for a moment. "Bein' so close to Halloween, I'll hold my tongue for now on all the trick-or-treat festivities in just about ever church around here. I reckon pastors can claim ignorance on the pagan influence of Easter eggs and Christmas trees, but it takes less sense than you'd find in the south end of a north-bound mule to figure out that Halloween is of the Devil. And I don't care how you Christianize it, dressin' up and trick-or-treatin' is a celebration of the Devil's day.

"But, folks don't want the little Christian children to miss out on anything, feel like weirdos and all. I reckon it's a good thing they's in America. I doubt many of 'em'd stand up for Jesus in North Korea or Saudi Arabia if they ain't willin' to give up a plastic bucket full of high-fructose corn syrup."

He shook his head as if frustrated. "Anyhow, I'm goin' to get back on topic. In the Revelation, Jesus dictates a letter to the church in Pergamum. He starts out by tellin' 'em what a fine job they've done in not denying His name. Then He hauls 'em off behind the woodshed. He speaks of the doctrine of Balaam.

"I'm sure y'all are quite familiar with the story of Balaam, but as a refresher, he was the prophet in the Book of Numbers. When the children of Israel came upon the land of Moab, ol' King Balak tried to hire Balaam to put a curse on the children of Israel. Well, Balaam asked the Lord and found that this people stretched out before Moab was the chosen people and could not be cursed. But that ol' Balak, bein' the devil that he was, begged Balaam, offerin' him all the riches his greedy little heart could desire. Balaam knew it weren't no doin', but he got to schemin' and devised a deception with which ol' Balak could use to lure the children of Israel out from under the protective hand of God. He told Balak that if'n he could get the Moabite women to entice the Israelite men into fornicatin' with 'em, them ol' boys'd be suckers for bowin' down to the Moabite gods. And sure enough, them boys fell for it, hook, line, and sinker.

"Besides the fornicatin', Jesus says in the Revelation that Balaam's scheme had them ol' boys eatin' food sacrificed to idols. He warns the church of Pergamum to repent, else He'd come and fight against them with the Sword of His mouth.

"Paul talks about eatin' foods sacrificed to idols in his epistle to the Corinthians. He says that those who do such are partakers in the pagan altars on which that food was sacrificed.

"I ain't just talkin' about eatin' trick-or-treats, although that might be the most obvious of all the foods sacrificed on a pagan altar that Christians do so readily partake. And I ain't just talking about Easter eggs, which are pagan symbols of worship to the fertility goddess Ashtar, nor the worship of Tammuz by erectin' Christmas trees. But I'm also talkin' about them filthy Hollywood movies and them pornographic TV shows that Christians run to watch, all the while happily enduring the offense as the name of their God is used as a curse word."

Pritchard shook his finger at the congregation in an almost-accusatory fashion. "I tell you what, them Muslims'd burn Hollywood to the ground if'n they was to misuse the name of Allah like that."

Pritchard stared silently at the small audience for a while. "I could stand here all day and preach against the sins of America; abortion, drunkenness, atheism bein' taught to our children by the government schools, all this queer business people's into these days—but don't none of it make a hill of beans if the church won't purify herself and turn back to God. Wherefore come out from among them, and be ye separate, saith the Lord, and touch not the unclean thing; and I will receive you.

"Jeremiah warns of the judgment of God coming upon Israel for her backsliding and idolatry. Ezekiel and Micah issue warnings to the faithless pastors who are full of compromise and complacency and work only for a paycheck.

"All these sins apply to America, but in the second chapter of Joel, God only makes one plea for the nation of Israel that they might be healed. He says, therefore also now, saith the Lord, turn ye even to me with all your heart, and with fasting, and with weeping, and with mourning: and rend your heart, and not your garments, and turn unto the Lord your God: for he is gracious and merciful, slow to anger, and of great kindness, and repenteth him of the evil. Who knoweth if he will return and repent, and leave a blessing behind him; even a meat offering and a drink offering unto the Lord your God?

"Blow the trumpet in Zion, sanctify a fast, call a solemn assembly: gather the people, sanctify the congregation, assemble the elders, gather the children, and those that suck the breasts: let the bridegroom go forth of his chamber, and the bride out of her closet. Let the priests, the ministers of the Lord, weep between the porch and the altar, and let them say, Spare thy people, O Lord, and give not thine heritage to reproach, that the heathen should rule over them: wherefore should they say among the people, Where is their God? Then will the Lord be jealous for his land, and pity his people. Yea, the Lord will answer and say unto his people, Behold, I will send you corn, and wine, and oil, and ye shall be satisfied therewith: and I will no more make you a reproach among the heathen.

"This right here, comin' together to worship Him with our whole hearts. If you do that, the rest takes care of itself. The Lord Jesus said all the law hangs on two little ol' commandments. Love the Lord your God with all your heart, mind, and soul. Then, love your neighbor as yourself.

"If you do that, you'll be covered. But if you don't, it don't matter that you cut out your drinkin'. You'll just replace it with fornicatin'. You'll cut out your gamblin' only to take to adultery.

"If you love God with your whole heart, you'll want to come to church, read your Bible, and you won't want to do those things which'll break His heart."

"I'm goin' to invite any of you who wants to come up here and dedicate your life to lovin' the Father, Son, and Holy Spirit with your whole heart. Maybe you said the magic prayer once long ago, but you didn't have no commitment. Come on up here and do it right.

"I ain't sayin' there's nothin' wrong with goin' up front and gettin' saved. But it's akin to gettin' hitched. If'n you was to run down the aisle and say 'I do' to some feller or gal, that's the first step in getting married. But if you didn't never go on no honeymoon, or move in together, nor see each other 'cept on Christmas and Easter, I think a lot of folk would question whether or not you was ever hitched in the first place."

"We ain't got no organ to play no sappy music, so if'n you want to dedicate your life to the Lord Jesus, you just come on up here."

Kate felt a strong sense of conviction in the pit of her stomach. It was as if Pritchard had written this whole thing just for her. She looked with surprise to see Terry standing. With tears streaming down his face, he marched to the front and stood near the tree trunk. Sam followed him and put his arm around his father.

"Aunt Kate?" Vicky had tears in her eyes also.

Kate held Vicky's hand and they walked down front. Nearly all in attendance left their seats to stand before the old man.

Pritchard's eyes were filled with surprise. "Ahhh, to tell y'all the truth, I didn't figure on none of youns comin' down. Guess I was countin' on my own strength and not the Spirit of the Lord. Well, anyhow, I ain't got nothin' prepared for you to say, so best just get on with tellin' Him whatever it is on your mind."

Kate bowed her head and poured out her heart to God in silent prayer. Others around her whispered their prayers.

After it was over, Kate went up to Mr. Pritchard. "Looks like you're a preacher after all."

He still looked shocked at the outcome. "Had to be the most convoluted thing I ever said. I can't take no credit for it. That was all the Lord's doin'."

CHAPTER 25

As a dog returneth to his vomit, so a fool returneth to his folly.

Proverbs 26:11

Kate's feeling of joy and enthusiasm came in for a hard landing no sooner than she returned home from the service. She watched Tina nudge Boyd, signaling for him to put out his cigarette. Kate marched up the stairs of the porch to where her brother and his girlfriend were sitting on the swing. "I see you found the stash."

"Oh, hey, Sis. What makes you say that?"

Kate looked at the yard behind Boyd. "The smoking cigarette on the ground and the fact that you're slurring your words. Sounds like you're half in the bag."

His eyes looked tired. "In all fairness, it was my stash to begin with."

Kate felt her blood beginning to boil, her jaw clenched.

Terry ascended the porch steps behind her. "Come on, let's get lunch going."

She exhaled and made a great mental effort to let go of the building rage. "Okay."

An hour later, Kate, Terry, and the kids sat around the quaint wooden table. Vicky asked, "Aunt Kate, can I borrow your Bible tonight? I've never read it and I feel like I should, like I want to."

"Sure. We can share it."

"Me, too, Aunt Kate?" Sam asked. "Maybe I can read it in the morning."

Terry said, "Dad's old Bible is around here somewhere. I'll dig it out after lunch. We're going to need more than one Bible for the house, it seems."

Kate pushed her plate to the side. "Did you meet any of the neighbors?" She glanced at her brother.

Terry had a pleasant expression on his face. "We did. Sam and I met Don and Mary Crisp. They're retired, moved up here from Orlando. We also met the Russos. Jack and Kelly. They have a daughter, Rainey, she just turned sixteen."

"The little brunette that was sitting to our right?" Kate asked.

"Yeah," replied Terry.

"She's cute, don't you think?" Kate looked at Sam.

He just shrugged and looked away.

Kate turned to Vicky. "Did you meet any of the neighbors?"

She beamed. "Maybe."

"No way! You hit on that kid?" Sam accused.

Vicky's brows snapped together. "I did not hit on him! For your information, he introduced himself to me! Then he introduced me to his parents, and his mom invited me to stop by one day this week. They're very nice people."

"Oh really?" Terry veiled his interrogation as dinner conversation. "What are his parents' names?"

"Scott and Amanda—McDowell, I think."

"Victoria McDowell," Sam teased. "It's not that different from Victoria McCarthy. You wouldn't even have to change homeroom in school."

"Shut up, Sam!" Vicky turned to her father. "Do you think we'll ever go back to school?"

Terry seemed so preoccupied by day-to-day survival that he didn't know how to answer. "Um… yeah." He gave an affirming nod. "Eventually. But it could be a while before things get back to normal."

"Mom's gone. It'll never be normal." Sam crossed his hands and looked down at the table.

Terry got up from his chair and stood by his son. "I know, but we'll get through this."

Kate looked at Vicky who was biting her lip as if to hold back the tears. She stood and held her arms open for her niece. Vicky got up and embraced her, burying her face in Kate's shoulder.

Kate hoped that Sam was wrong. She hoped normal would return someday.

Late Sunday night, Terry pushed Kate's door open. "I'm going to turn in. Are you good to go until 4:00 AM?"

"Yeah. Are the kids asleep?"

"Sam is. Vicky is still reading your Bible."

Kate asked, "Did you say anything to the neighbors about a block watch?"

Terry sighed. "I didn't want to throw that out there on the first conversation. I want to feel them out first, try to get a sense of where they're at in terms of accepting reality. Edith Ramsey is a prime example that people are all over the chart when it comes to understanding what's really going on."

Kate looked out the window into the cool night air. "That sounds wise."

"Besides," Terry added, "I didn't want to advertise the fact that our derelict brother is the one inviting trouble into Apple Blossom Acres."

"Yeah, we'd be pariahs for sure." Kate wished things were different, but they weren't.

"You've got the whistle?"

She held the stainless-steel object up by the cord around her neck. "Sam and Vicky both have pistols. They know to bring them here if they hear me blow it."

"Okay, I'll see you in a few hours."

"Okay." Kate gazed down at the butt of her shotgun.

Terry paused before closing the door. "Is there something else?"

She glanced up. "Do you think we should, like, you know—pray? I mean if we really believe what we claim, don't you think God will hear us? Don't you think it might help?"

Terry came in and closed the door behind him. He knelt by her bed and folded his hands. "Do you want to, or do you want me to?"

"You do it." She knelt beside him.

Terry said, "God, we thank you for your forgiveness and your mercy. I'm sorry we haven't made much time for you and I'm sorry things had to get so bad before we felt like we needed you. But we need you now. Watch over us tonight. We know it's a dangerous world, but we believe that you are bigger and more powerful than the terrors here. I pray especially that you'd keep my little sister, my boy, and my precious little girl safe in your arms. Amen."

Kate looked up. "Thanks."

He kissed her on the forehead. "I'll see you in a while."

Kate woke up to the sound of tires crunching the gravel in her driveway. "Oh no! I fell asleep. What's happening?" She peered out the window to see a pickup truck with its lights off backing up toward the garage. Six men with long guns were in the bed of the truck. She assumed at least two more were in the cab. Instinctively, she blew the whistle as hard as she could.

The men below bounded from the bed of the pickup and pointed their guns toward the house.

Another man stepped out of the passenger's seat and called out. "Two ways we can do this. The easy way or the hard way. The easy way is you open this garage door, and we load up our truck and leave."

Kate recognized the man as being one of the hooligans Boyd had brought to the house.

He continued, "The hard way, well, I think that's self-explanatory. But the short answer is that I've already left here once without taking what's coming to me. That ain't gonna happen again."

Terry came into the room. "What's happening?"

"Boyd's friends, they want our stuff." She stayed near the edge of the window.

Sam and Vicky arrived, both holding their pistols.

"If we give it to them, maybe they'll just leave." Vicky looked to her father.

"Then we'll starve. I'd rather get shot." Sam leaned over to peek out the window.

Kate looked at Terry. "Sam is right. That food in the garage is all that separates us from the people who are dying of starvation in the cities."

Terry pulled the curtain back to assess the situation below. "We're outgunned and outmanned."

"We have to try!" Kate tucked the .38 in her waistband and grabbed a box of shotgun shells, which had been modified as per Sam's recommendations.

Terry's lips were pressed tightly together. "What do you suggest?"

Kate thought quickly. "Sam and I will go to the garage and kill anyone who tries to come in the door. Do you feel like you could pick a couple off from up here with the deer rifle?"

Terry switched off the rifle's safety. "I think so."

Kate looked at Vicky. "I need you to be strong. You watch my bedroom door. If any of them try to come up the stairs, take them out. Knowing that he won't get ambushed from behind will allow your dad to focus on his mission. If he can take out three or four of them before they get in the house, it will even up the numbers and give us a fighting chance. Can you do that?"

Vicky's face was filled with terror. She swallowed hard and gave a faint nod.

Kate kissed her on the head. "I've got the whistle. If I blow it, that means they're inside the garage."

Kate looked at Sam. "Come on."

The two of them hustled down the stairs to the first floor where Tina was standing in the hall, eyes swollen and groggy. "What's going on?"

"Boyd's friends are back. Stay in your room and stay out of the way." Kate ran past her to the door which led to the basement.

"I told you that you should have just let it play out." Boyd stuck his head out the bedroom door.

"Shut up, Boyd." Kate led the way down the stairs.

"Can I at least have a gun?" Boyd called out behind her.

"No!" she yelled back.

Once at the bottom of the stairs, Kate slowly opened the door to the garage. She whispered, "Stay behind me."

A loud mechanical sound echoed in the garage, like a mini jackhammer. Kate pointed to the blade that was cutting through the metal door. "What's that?" she yelled over the noise of the machine.

"Looks like a Sawzall."

"A what?"

"A reciprocal saw," Sam replied.

A shot rang out from the other side of the door, then the sawing ceased.

Voices of the ruffians could be heard through the garage door. Kate heard the man who'd addressed them when they first arrived. "Looks like it's going to be the hard way. That's fine with me!"

His voice was followed by a volley of gunfire.

"They're shooting at Dad!" Sam yelled.

"Let's give him some cover." Kate took aim at the point in the garage where the man had been sawing. She fired the shotgun. BOOOM! The homemade slug left a single hole in the garage door.

Sam followed suit, firing several rounds from his .45.

Kate pumped the shotgun and fired again and again. She had no idea if the modified target loads were fragmenting after they left the garage door, but they consistently punched one single hole through the door for each shot.

"Justin is down!" called someone from outside.

Another yelped out, "I'm hit!"

Kate fired two more rounds, then began shoving fresh shells in the tubular magazine.

The man called out orders, "Chris, you focus on the sniper up top, the rest of you, light up that garage. I've got a little surprise for them."

Kate looked at Sam. "Get down and reload. We need to be ready for whatever they're coming at us with."

Sam took cover inside the basement door and switched magazines.

CHAPTER 26

I will call upon the Lord, who is worthy to be praised: so shall I be saved from mine enemies. The sorrows of death compassed me, and the floods of ungodly men made me afraid. The sorrows of hell compassed me about: the snares of death prevented me. In my distress I called upon the Lord, and cried unto my God: he heard my voice out of his temple, and my cry came before him, even into his ears.

Psalm 18:3-6

Kate listened to the continuing gunfire with one hand on her shotgun and the other on her nephew's shoulder. The shots fell silent. She looked at Sam with apprehension. The next sound was the engine of the truck revving up, then tires ripping through gravel, and finally, the loud crash of the pickup's tailgate smashing through the garage door.

She tugged Sam's shirt. "Come on, back upstairs!"

Sam stood but did not follow her directive. He began firing at the men rushing into the garage past the busted door.

"Now, Sam!" She grabbed his arm and pulled him back. Bullets whizzed by their heads.

"I got one of them, Aunt Kate!" He reluctantly followed.

"And they nearly killed us both." She charged up two flights of stairs to her room where Vicky stood guarding the door.

"Come on! Hurry!" Vicky stepped back to let them in.

Kate slammed the door behind her. "They're in the house."

"I kinda figured that." Terry loaded more bullets into the .270. "We gotta keep fighting." He popped up again into the open window and took another shot.

"How many are left?" Kate asked.

"I've killed two and one of them got hit from you two shooting through the garage door."

Sam added. "I shot one inside the garage also."

"I think we started with eight. We should be fairly well evened up by now." Kate listened through the door to hear if the attackers were coming up the stairs.

Terry again took aim through the upstairs window and fired a shot. POW! Crack, Crack, Crack! Semi-automatic rifle fire rang out from below. Terry spun around, landing face down on the wood floor.

"Daddy!" Vicky turned him over to reveal blood staining his shirt.

"Sam, go to my bathroom and get some towels." Kate quickly pulled Terry's shirt up so she could assess the wound.

Sam soon returned with the towels. "They're coming up the stairs."

Kate gave the towels to Vicky who was sobbing uncontrollably. "Keep pressure on the wound."

Vicky wiped her tears with the back of her hand and took the towels.

Kate took aim down the stairs, fired at one of the men, then racked a fresh shell into the chamber. She turned to her brother who was badly wounded. "Terry, you're going to be okay."

He remained on the ground. "Sam, take the rifle, son. Keep your sister and your aunt safe."

Sam's eyes were filled with tears. He took the rifle. "I love you, Dad."

"And I love you, son." He looked at Vicky who was holding the bloody towel against his chest. "And you'll always be my precious little girl."

She wailed in anguish, "I love you, Daddy. Don't die!"

His voice was shallow. "You're going to be okay. You've got your aunt and your brother. You'll get through this. You're stronger than you think."

Kate choked back her sorrow. She had to survive the assault.

"Come out, come out, wherever you are!" The voice of the man who'd been at the house with Boyd called out in a sing-song voice.

Kate grimaced with internal torment. Perhaps if she'd let the deal go through, this wouldn't be happening. Or, perhaps they'd have come back to rob them anyway. Regardless, there was no going back. What was done was done.

Vicky yelled through the door. "Just take the food and leave."

"Oh, no. That deal expired when you shot my men. This is all about revenge now." The man laughed loudly. "I guess there's one other way we could settle this."

"What's that?" Kate asked.

"We're a little short on female companionship back at the house, if you know what I mean. If you girls want to surrender, I'm sure we could make an exception. The fellas though, they've gotta go."

Kate fumed with anger, calculated where the voice was coming from, and fired through the door.

Return fire echoed up the stairs. Bullets ripped through the interior walls and the door.

Kate pulled her niece and nephew to the ground. "Get down!"

"Aunt Kate, they have AK-47's. Besides that, all of our extra ammo is in the garage. We can't compete." Sam sounded like he was ready to give up.

Kate pulled them behind the bed and lay prone with the shotgun pointed at the door. "We have no choice, Sam. We have to keep fighting."

"I know. I'm just saying, maybe we should just storm down the stairs and take as many of them with us as we can."

"No. It's not over until it's over. We're not going on any suicide mission either." She swallowed hard.

The man yelled out, "That wasn't very neighborly of you, taking a shot at me like that. I'm going to give the ladies one last chance, then we're coming in, and you're all going to die."

Sam looked at his aunt. "All four of the remaining men are in the house. What if I distract them so you and Vicky can escape out the window?"

She put her hand on his arm. "That's very brave, Sam. But I'm going to see this thing through, no matter what."

Sam looked at his sister. "Vicky, do you want to try to get away?"

She wiped the tears from her eyes, shook her head and pointed her pistol at the door.

The man called out once more. "Ready or not!"

Bullets peppered through the door and wall, sending bits of drywall and wood raining down on Kate and the kids. Sam and Vicky both returned fire. Kate waited to see a target before shooting.

The gunfire stopped. "I'm out!" Vicky whispered.

"Me, too." Sam's voice was filled with distress.

"Take my pistol, Vicky. "Sam, get your dad's revolver." Kate handed the .38 to her niece. "And don't shoot until you have a target in your sight."

The man said mockingly from downstairs,

"Sounds like you might be about out of ammo. Maybe you gals will be coming back with us after all."

Vicky looked at Kate, her eyes filled with utter remorse. "I can't do that, Aunt Kate. If I run out of bullets... I'm saving one for myself. Please forgive me."

Kate couldn't stand the situation they were in. With her entire heart, she wished she could go back in time, put more of the ammo upstairs, and have better weapons for defense. She gently put the back of her hand on Vicky's cheek. "I understand." She considered the horrible option for herself, wondering how she could get the barrel of the shotgun to her mouth in her current position.

"Fee-fi-fo-fum." The man stomped up the stairs. "Kick it open, Edmond."

"Why me?"

"They ain't got no bullets left, just do it!" another man demanded.

CRASH! The door flew open. Kate, Vicky, and Sam fired simultaneously. The man flew backward, clearing the way for the other three ruffians to shoot into the room. Kate and the kids continued shooting for another several seconds. The house fell silent once more.

Sam pulled the trigger of the revolver and it clicked. "Are you out?"

"I've got one more shell," Kate replied.

"Me, too." Vicky held the .38 with both hands.

"I'm bettin' you're empty now," the man said angrily.

"Why don't you come on in here and see," Kate

yelled in fury.

"Aunt Kate…" Vicky shook her head. "We've got two shots left. There's three of the men still out there. This isn't going to end well." She put the pistol under her chin.

Sam cried, "No Vicky, you can't leave me!"

Kate felt utterly crushed by the circumstance. She was beyond despair, past brokenhearted, fear had her in a chokehold. She couldn't think, couldn't decide what to do with her last shell, had no idea what to say to her niece who was about to take her own life in a last-ditch effort to avoid the unfathomable.

Gunfire rang out. Kate readied herself for the inevitable; with her final shotgun shell, she'd kill the next person who came through that door. And if the others took her, she'd claw their eyes out with her fingernails before she let them take her alive.

The gunfire continued for some time, rising and falling in intensity. Kate forced herself to look at her niece to see if she was still alive. Vicky had a perplexed look on her face but still held the pistol snuggly beneath her jaw.

Then, the unavoidable happened. The man who'd haunted Kate since she first saw him in the garage with Boyd came into her bedroom. Oddly, he didn't come in shooting, rather he knelt down inside her door and looked out. Nevertheless, she didn't hesitate. She placed the bead of the shotgun over the back of his head and pulled the trigger. BOOM!

Sam snatched the pistol from Vicky before she could fire her weapon.

"No! Sam! Please, you don't know what they'll

do to me!"

He stood up in the doorway with the pistol. "The next one through this door won't be the one to do it."

Kate admired her nephew's courage but knew Vicky's fate would be a bad one if she didn't get away. She pushed her out from behind the bed. "Vicky, get out the window. Hang by your fingers then drop down. Let your knees bend when you hit the drive so you don't break a leg. Then run. Go to Mr. Pritchard's house and hide. There's only two left. Let your brother and me deal with them."

Vicky sobbed and threw her arms around Kate's neck.

Kate kissed her and then pushed her away. "You have to go. You have to go now!"

"I love you, Sam." Vicky put one foot slowly out the window.

"I love you, too. Now go!" Sam's hands trembled waiting to fire the final shot.

"Girl? Are you still up there?"

"Mr. Pritchard?" Kate couldn't believe what she was hearing.

"Kate?" Another familiar voice came from below.

"Gavin!" She let the empty shotgun fall to the ground. Quickly she turned to see Vicky's fingers hanging from the window sill. "Sam, help me get Vicky back inside. I think we're going to be okay."

Sam tucked the pistol in his waist. He grabbed one hand while Kate grabbed the other. The two of them pulled Vicky up and helped her back inside.

"What's going on?" Vicky asked.

Kate wasn't certain, but she said, "Everything is going to be okay."

Sam took the pistol back out of his belt but held it low.

Gavin came into the room with an AK-47 hanging from a sling around his shoulder. He held up one hand to Sam. "Easy there big fella. We're on the same side."

Sam looked at Kate. "Do you know this guy?"

Filled with relief and deep sadness over her brother, Kate fell into Gavin's open arms. She cried long and hard, letting the tears she'd been holding back flow freely onto his firm shoulder.

Pritchard walked into the room with his shotgun pointed at the floor. "I don't know what you shot that heathen layin' in the doorway with, but you 'bout blew his head clean off his neck."

Kate was in no mood to discuss details with the old man. She had no idea how she'd get through the coming days without her brother, but she knew she had to; for Sam and Vicky's sakes. She looked over to where Terry lay motionless on the floor. Vicky sat beside him, tears streaming down both cheeks. Sam was behind her, his arms wrapped around his sister and his face contorted in soul-wrenching pain.

"Where's that no-account brother of your'n?" Pritchard surveyed the room.

Kate looked around. She broke free from Gavin's embrace and looked out the window. "I'm not sure."

"Why don't you take the youngins and go look for him. Ain't no need of them seein' their pa like this. I'll get him cleaned up and laid out proper like.

We'll have a good service for him. And we'll all get through this." The old man nodded with determination. "Best take this young man with y'all. Can't be too sure there ain't none of them devils still about."

Gavin changed magazines. "I'll make sure they're safe."

"Very well. Once you know it to be true, come on back up here and give me a hand fixin' up their pa."

"It should be me," Kate said. "I'll help you with Terry."

"Suit yourself." Pritchard began collecting the bloody towels from the floor. "I reckon this young fella can help getting' the other corpses cleared out of your house. 'Fraid we made a mess of things."

Kate let Gavin put his arm around her. "I appreciate you showing up when you did, Mr. Pritchard." She took Gavin's hand in hers. "And you, too. I don't know what would have happened if you hadn't."

CHAPTER 27

A friend loveth at all times, and a brother is born for adversity.

Proverbs 17:17

Kate held out her hand to Sam. "Let me hang on to the .38. We'll go down to the garage first and reload all our weapons, then we'll look for your uncle. Once we find Boyd, we'll take half the ammo upstairs to my room. I don't want to get caught like that again. I know you're both tired and grieving, but I should have done this when I first bought the bullets."

Sam nodded. He seemed to understand that work still needed to be done before he could mourn his father's death.

Kate led the way down two flights of stairs to

the garage with Gavin close behind her. Once the guns were reloaded, they headed back up to the main level. Kate pushed open the door to Boyd's room. "Boyd? Are you in here?"

Gavin looked under the bed. "No one here."

Kate pressed her lips together tightly. "This closet goes back under the stairs. We used to hide there as kids." She opened the door and pushed the hanging clothes to the side. "You can come out. Your friends are all dead... and so is your brother."

Boyd crawled over some boxes that he'd positioned to hide behind, then helped Tina out of the closet. "I knew something bad would happen when you interrupted that deal."

Kate blew a fuse. "Why can't you accept the least amount of responsibility for bringing those goons here in the first place? What is wrong with you, Boyd? Are you so blind, so delusional, or are you just in denial?"

"I'll accept my part of the blame if you'll accept yours."

"Get out! Right now! Both of you. Pack your bags and leave this instant."

"Whoa! This isn't your house. You can't throw me out."

"You're right! It's mine and Terry's. But since he's dead, I'm calling the shots. Now get out!"

"Terry's part goes to his kids. Since he was two-thirds owner, they each have as much say in the matter as you." Boyd looked at his niece and nephew with puppy-dog eyes. "They won't kick me out into the cold night."

Kate could take no more. "These kids have been

through enough because of you. I won't have you manipulating them."

"I want to hear what they've got to say." He crossed his arms and tilted his chin up ever so slightly.

"They're minors. And since they have no father and no mother, I'm responsible for keeping them safe. They'll never be safe as long as you're around."

"Responsibility—oh, I see." His voice dripped with sarcasm. "And what court decided you're the legal guardian? Seems I'm just as much of a blood relative as you. What if I decide I want custody?"

She pulled her pistol. "Go, Boyd."

"You won't pull that trigger. You wouldn't shoot your own brother."

Gavin leveled his AK-47 at Boyd. "You're probably right, but I will."

"Oh, that'd be real convenient for you, wouldn't it?" Boyd's voice was filled with insolence.

"Not really. I was hoping to come up here for a relaxing visit. But instead, I rolled up on a full-fledged firefight. Convenient would have been for me to turn around and go right back down that mountain. Instead, I risked my neck and nearly got killed. And I take it from the context of the conversation that this is all your fault. Does that sound about right?"

Sam pulled the hammer back on his .45, aiming at Boyd's head. "I should be the one to kill him. He got Dad shot, and it's my duty to take him out."

"No, Sam!" Kate called out. "Uncle Boyd is going to leave. No one has to kill him. But if he doesn't, Gavin will be the one to do it. Boyd's your uncle, and you don't want to live with that." She turned to Tina. "Seems like people are getting ready to draw straws over who gets to put Boyd out of our misery. If you have any sense at all, you'll get him out of here while the getting's good."

"Come on, Boyd, let's go." Tina tugged his arm.

"At least let us take some food. Otherwise, we're dead anyways." Boyd held his hands up.

"No, you've taken enough." Kate clenched her jaw.

"Then just shoot me. It'll be less painful than starving to death." Boyd gave a crooked smile as if issuing a dare.

Gavin raised his rifle.

"No! Aunt Kate. Let him have some food. I can't watch anyone else get killed. Please!" Vicky cried.

"One bucket," Kate said.

"Six. We need at least enough food for a month."

Kate shook her head. "No way. Vicky, go upstairs. Gavin, wait until she's out of the room, then kill him."

"Wait!" Tina screamed with her hands up. "What about two buckets? That's about a week's worth of food each. Please, Boyd! Say that's good. I don't want to die."

"Two buckets?" Boyd looked at Kate with his arms crossed.

"I'll pick the buckets. Gavin, keep your rifle on him until he's gone." Kate turned to go to the garage. She grabbed one bucket of rice and one bucket of beans, each with bullet holes which leaked a trail of dried beans and rice behind her.

Kate took them back to the living room. "Take it and go."

"We need gas." Boyd protested.

"Vicky, upstairs!" Kate pointed. "Gavin..."

Tina grabbed the buckets and headed for the door. "We have a quarter tank. Come on, Boyd!"

Boyd bit his lip and shook his head. He walked out the door behind Tina. "I'm glad Dad's not alive to see this."

"Me, too!" Kate slammed the door behind Boyd and Tina.

Boyd made one final protest before leaving the property. "That was the Badger Creek Gang you started a feud with. And Jason Graves was one of the leaders. His brother won't be too happy to find out Jason's dead. Good luck with all that." Tina's BMW kicked rocks when they pulled out of the driveway.

Vicky shook her head. "Uncle Boyd has been here less than two weeks. He couldn't have learned everything there is to know about the local organized crime gang in that amount of time. He's just trying to frighten us."

Kate locked the deadbolt. "Your uncle has a special talent for meeting all the wrong sort of people." She looked up at Pritchard. "Have you heard of the Badger Creek Gang?"

"Yep. Nasty bunch."

Sam inquired, "What about the brother? Is what Uncle Boyd said true?"

The old man's face was grim. "'Fraid so. But if they come, we'll be ready for 'em. Don't you worry none."

As the anger and fear subsided, sorrow returned to Kate's heart. Still, she had a job to do. She'd try to get the kids to go to bed, then help Pritchard with getting Terry's body cleaned up. Even after that was done, the house was covered in blood, shattered walls, shot-up doors, and empty shell casings. Just thinking about everything that needed to be done sapped what little strength she had left.

Once she and Pritchard finished with Terry and got him laid out on the bed, the old man said, "Why don't you go get yourself washed up? Then take an hour or two to rest. The sun will be up soon, and it's goin' to be a hard day for you and them youngins."

Kate looked around. "But this mess!"

"Don't you worry about that. That boy's about got all the bodies dragged out of the house. Ever thing else can wait."

She let out a sigh of capitulation. "Maybe just an hour or two." She took a long hot shower then reclined on her bed. "Just an hour or two."

CHAPTER 28

A fire devoureth before them; and behind them a flame burneth: the land is as the garden of Eden before them, and behind them a desolate wilderness; yea, and nothing shall escape them. The appearance of them is as the appearance of horses; and as horsemen, so shall they run. Like the noise of chariots on the tops of mountains shall they leap, like the noise of a flame of fire that devoureth the stubble, as a strong people set in battle array. Before their face the people shall be much pained: all faces shall gather blackness.

They shall run like mighty men; they shall climb the wall like men of war; and they shall march every one on his ways, and they shall not break their ranks: Neither shall one thrust another; they shall walk every one in his path: and when they fall upon the sword, they shall not be wounded. They shall run to and fro in the city; they shall run upon the wall, they shall climb up upon the houses; they shall enter in at the windows like a thief.

The earth shall quake before them; the heavens shall tremble: the sun and the moon shall be dark, and the stars shall withdraw their shining: And the Lord shall utter his voice before his army: for his camp is very great: for he is strong that executeth his word: for the day of the Lord is great and very terrible; and who can abide it?

Joel 2:3-11

Kate awoke to a gentle touch on her hand. She looked up to see Gavin gazing at her tenderly. "What time is it?" She sat up.

"5:00," he said.

She looked out the window at the waning sun. "In the evening?"

"Yeah. Sam and Vicky are up. I didn't want to wake you, but Mr. Pritchard said we need to have a burial service for Terry today. Otherwise…"

"I know." She needed no explanation, and she

certainly didn't want the kids to see their father once the next stage of decomposition set in.

She looked at his rifle propped up in the corner. "Did you bring that AK-47 with you?'"

"Yeah. I think I mentioned that I was going to look into getting a better gun."

Her brows pulled close. "You did, but you didn't mention an AK-47."

"They didn't have any Hemlock BF-Rs in stock at the gun store."

She replied, "Probably because that gun only exists in Titanfall."

"Yeah, so I went with the runner-up. It's always been my go-to gun in any video game where it's available. And now you have one."

"I have an AK-47?"

"To the victor go the spoils. Five of the guys who hit your house were carrying AKs. You also picked up another shotgun, and two AR-15s."

"I don't know how to use any of them except the shotgun."

"I can walk you through the AK at least."

"Where did you learn to shoot?"

"The gun range. I took it out as soon as I bought it. A couple of older guys at the range walked me through the basics. Then I practiced as much as I could. What about you? Seems like you at least know how to pull the trigger."

"My dad, he taught me basic gun safety and how to fire a shotgun when I was a kid. It came back pretty fast. What about ammo? Did the intruders leave any behind?"

"Seems they spent most of it, but I'd say you

have a thousand rounds that they left behind."

"I guess we'll need it, especially if this gang decides to give us any trouble." Kate pulled her hair back and sighed. She took Gavin's hand and pulled it close. "So, what made you decide to stop by?"

"I would have called, but cell service went out in Charlotte a few days ago."

"Well, I'm glad you came."

Gavin smiled. "Pretty good timing on my part, if I do say so myself."

She put her other hand on his and pulled him closer. "Not just because you saved my life, although I am grateful for that. So, cell service is completely out?"

He squeezed her hands. "I think the government shut it down because it was doing more harm than good. Gangs and hoodlums were using it to organize."

"What about first responders?"

He shook his head. "They're all responding to their own personal crisis. Things got pretty rough in Charlotte. I holed up in my apartment for as long as I could. Fortunately, my Jeep didn't get vandalized. I decided to get out while I still could. I have a cousin in Tennessee; Whiteville, it's pretty remote. I wanted to stop by and make sure you were okay before I went."

"Oh." Kate felt like she'd had the wind knocked out of her. She pulled back one of her hands and looked down at the quilt. "I see. When are you leaving?"

"I'd told Mr. Pritchard that I'd help get things back in order around here. We've been at it hard.

We've got most of it cleaned up, but I'm beat. If you don't mind, I'd like to crash here, on the couch or something. I need to get some rest before I go. I was thinking of heading out after midnight tomorrow night. Early morning hours seem to be the safest time to travel."

"Sure, you can sleep here." She felt despondent.

"Is everything okay? I mean, I know you've been through a lot, but you seem upset at me. If you'd rather I not stay…"

"No." She looked up. "It's not you, it's me. I don't know why, but I had it cooked up in my mind that you'd be staying longer. No reason, just my imagination, I guess."

He bit his lip. "Why? How long did you think I was going to stay?"

She lifted her shoulders and looked away, her heart began to pound. "I don't know, a while."

"What's a while? A couple days?"

She fiddled with the edge of the quilt. "I don't know, maybe longer."

"Do you *want* me to stay longer?"

She looked up into his eyes and nodded.

"I could hang around for a while."

"How long is a while?" she asked.

He laughed and pulled her close. "You tell me."

Despite her fear, her worry, and her grief, a smile began to creep across her face.

Gavin put his hand behind her neck and softly pulled her closer for a kiss.

Seconds later, she pulled away, still smiling and looked away. "So, were you really going to Tennessee, or was that just to make me beg?"

"I hadn't exactly been invited, so I wasn't about to impose myself upon you."

"But it's the apocalypse. One could assume that one's company would be welcome."

"Mmmm..." He tilted his head to the side. "One could, and one might; but personally, I need a formal invitation."

She sat up straight in the bed and took both of his hands. "Okay, Gavin, will you please come stay with me? I'm a fair maiden in distress, and I could really use a knight in shining armor."

He grinned. "I don't know if I'm buying all that fair-maiden bit."

"Oh? I'm not fair?"

"Fair, indeed, my princess, but in distress? I saw that guy's face where you shot him—or at least what used to be his face. Nevertheless, I accept your invitation to stay for..."

"A while—a good long while." She let him kiss her again.

Thanks for reading *Cyber Armageddon, Book One: Rise of the Locusts*

Reviews are the best way to help get the book noticed. If you liked the book, please take a moment to leave a five-star review on Amazon and Goodreads.

I love hearing from readers! So whether it's to say you enjoyed the book, to point out a typo that we missed, or asked to be notified when new books are released, drop me a line.
prepperrecon@gmail.com

Stay tuned to **PrepperRecon.com** for the latest news about my upcoming books.

If you've enjoyed *Rise of the Locusts*, you'll love my end-times thriller series, ***The Days of Noah***

In an off-site CIA facility outside of Langley, rookie analyst Everett Carroll discovers he's not being told the whole truth. He's instructed to disregard troubling information uncovered by his research. Everett ignores his directive and keeps digging. What he finds goes against everything he's been taught to believe. Unfortunately, his curiosity doesn't escape the attention of his superiors, and it may cost him his life.

Meanwhile, Tennessee public school teacher, Noah Parker, like many in the United States, has been asleep at the wheel. During his complacency, the founding precepts of America have been systematically destroyed by a conspiracy that dates back hundreds of years.

Cassandra Parker, Noah's wife, has diligently followed end-times prophecy and the shifting tide against freedom in America. Noah has tried to avoid the subject, but when charges are filed against him for deviating from the approved curriculum in his school, he quickly understands the seriousness of the situation. The signs can no longer be ignored, and Noah is forced to prepare for the cataclysmic period of financial and political upheaval ahead.

Watch through the eyes of Noah Parker and Everett Carroll as the world descends into chaos, a global empire takes shape, ancient writings are fulfilled, and the last days fall upon the once-great United States of America.

If you have an affinity for the prophetic don't miss my EMP survival series, ***Seven Cows, Ugly and Gaunt***

In ***Book One: Behold Darkness and Sorrow***, Daniel Walker begins having prophetic dreams about the judgment coming upon America for rejecting God. Through one of his dreams, Daniel learns of an imminent threat of an EMP attack which will wipe out America's electric grid and most all computerized devices, sending the country into a technological dark age.

Living in a nation where all life-sustaining systems of support are completely dependent on electricity and computers, the odds of survival are dismal. Municipal water services, retail food distribution, police, fire, EMS and all emergency services will come to a screeching halt.

If they want to live, Daniel and his friends must focus on faith, wits, and preparation to be ready . . . before the lights go out.

You'll also enjoy my series about the coming civil war in America, *Ava's Crucible*

The deck is stacked against twenty-nine-year-old Ava. She's a fighter, but she's got trust issues and doesn't always make the best decisions. Her personal complications aren't without merit, but America is on the verge of a second civil war, and Ava must pull it together if she wants to survive.

The tentacles of the deep state have infiltrated every facet of American culture. The public education system, entertainment industry, and mainstream media have all been hijacked by a shadow government intent on fomenting a communist revolution in the United States. The antagonistic message of this agenda has poisoned the minds of America's youth who are convinced that capitalism and conservatism are responsible for all the ills of the world. Violent protest, widespread destruction, and politicians who insist on letting the disassociated vent their rage will bring America to her knees, threatening to decapitate the laws, principles, and values on which the country was founded. The revolution has been well-planned, but the socialists may have underestimated America's true patriots who refuse to give up without a fight.

ABOUT THE AUTHOR

Mark Goodwin holds a degree in accounting and monitors macroeconomic conditions to stay up-to-date with the ongoing global meltdown. He is an avid student of the Holy Bible and spends several hours every week devoted to the study of Scripture and the prophecies contained therein. The troubling trends in the moral, social, political, and financial landscapes have prompted Mark to conduct extensive research within the arena of preparedness. He weaves his knowledge of biblical prophecy, economics, politics, prepping, and survival into an action-packed tapestry of post-apocalyptic fiction. Having been a sinner saved by grace himself, the story of redemption is a prominent theme in all of Mark's writings.

"He brought me up also out of an horrible pit, out of the miry clay, and set my feet upon a rock, and established my goings." Psalm 40:2

Made in the USA
Columbia, SC
14 January 2020